AFTER I WAS HIS

AFTER I WAS HIS

AMELIA WILDE

Cover Design: Coverlüv

Cover Model: Chris Burgess

Photographer: Alex Wightman Photography

For heroes everywhere

1

THE BEST MAN IS MISSING.

Not *missing persons report* missing, I hope, but he's not here in Houston Hall. I've gathered as much from the mother of the bride, one Linda Sullivan. The bride is my best friend and former roommate, Summer. It is *her day.*

I was only three mimosas into this glorious event when Linda grabbed me by the elbow and pulled me into a little alcove, hiding us from the caterers behind a potted plant. "My son is missing," she said urgently. "He's not here."

I wanted to make a joke about where men *usually* are when things get serious, but weddings, as I've learned from life experience, are *not* the place for jokes until the reception gets to that boozy point in the evening when nobody can remember what you say or if you were even there. I nodded solemnly and asked the obvious question. "Any idea where he might be?"

"No. Dayton went to his room at the hotel and there was no answer."

"Did he check the hotel bar?"

"Of course he checked—why would Wes be at the hotel bar? This is his sister's wedding day. He wouldn't be *drinking*."

"No, of course not," I said, trying to contain the eye roll I so desperately wanted to let loose.

"We have to tell Summer."

"Do we *have* to tell her? As the bride, she should probably be sheltered from such pedestrian troubles as—"

"We're telling Summer," Linda said fiercely. "If we have to delay the pictures, she deserves an explanation."

"Aren't the pictures happening at, like, any moment?"

"Yes," she said slowly, as if I was mildly stupid. "That's why we have to tell her now."

"Go ahead. I'll be right behind you."

Linda gives me a look colder than ice. Down the hall, Hazel, Summer's bridesmaid, floats toward the bridal suite, looking every bit a redheaded supermodel. Linda turned her head and waved frantically to her. "Hazel," she hissed. "Hazel, we've got a problem."

Now that Hazel has been brought up to speed, it's time to approach the bride.

We enter the bridal suite *en masse*, the both of us flanking Mrs. Sullivan, who actually looks quite stately in a shimmering silver mother-of-the-bride gown that doesn't make her look old as hell. Hazel and I are in matching sage green numbers.

Summer stands up at the sight of us, her too-cute baby

January squirming in her arms. They're both disgustingly beautiful, even if January is *way* underdressed for the occasion. She's only wearing a diaper. "Thank God, Mom. We've got to get me in this dress." Summer's dress hangs by the window, framed by her shoes and jewelry. It was a whole thing for the photographer.

"Are you sure about this?" I mumble out of the corner of my mouth. All three of us in the bridal party look at each other.

Linda doesn't answer.

"Oh, no," Summer says. "What's the look for?"

More silence from stately Linda, who looks at her daughter with tears filling her eyes. I'd get choked up myself if I hadn't already been over every detail of Summer's wedding ensemble with her every day for the last month. Her blonde hair tumbles down over her shoulders, brought back and pinned with antique hair pieces, tiny pearls glinting off the edges. She looks like a princess in yoga pants. With the dress on, she'll be a total stunner.

"Mom? Did something happen?"

I will Linda to get this over with, so we can move on to solving the problem and back to the joyous, festive atmosphere that is everyone's wedding day.

"You—" Linda presses her fingertips to her lips. "You look absolutely gorgeous, Sunny."

All this, and she doesn't even have the dress on yet. I shove down an ugly curl of jealousy at the pit of my gut.

"Thanks, Mom. Really."

This has gone on too long. Now that we're here, about to

pull the trigger, Linda is losing her nerve. It's my turn to step in.

"There's a slight issue," I say, trying to make my face look both lighthearted and comforting. I have no idea if I'm pulling it off. Summer's eyebrows raise. This is code for, *Tell me what's wrong immediately, and why have you phrased it like this? Maximum suspense? You're an asshole, Whitney.* "With your brother."

"With Wes?" Summer's eyebrows draw closer together, her entire forehead wrinkling. "What's wrong with Wes?"

January reaches up and tugs at one of Summer's curls. Summer cups her tiny hand in her own and gives it a kiss. The gesture is so habitual, so natural, that it grips a bit at my heart.

I started this, and I'm going to finish it. "We can't find him."

"What do you mean, you can't find him?"

Linda finally finds her voice. "He's...not in the hotel," she says. Is she relishing this? The way we're all hanging on every word? "Dayton went up to his room, and—"

"Day's not here, is he?" Summer cranes her neck to look behind us. "He's not supposed to see me until the first look. Tell me he's not here."

"Heeeyyyy," says January, interrupting us with a gummy smile. Damn, she's cute. I give her a little wave. Then I snap out of it.

"He's not here," I say confidently, though the man could be striding into the room right now. "We just wanted to...update you on the situation."

"We're working on finding him, Sunny, so don't worry about it."

Summer gives her mother a pleading look. "You're going to find him, right?"

"Right. Of course."

Summer closes her eyes and takes in a deep breath, then opens them again. "Any other disasters are on a need-to-know basis, okay? Whit?"

"It wasn't my idea," I tell her, which earns me a sloppily disguised side-eye from Linda. "But that's totally irrelevant. I'm going to find Wes right now."

"Yes. Whitney is going to find Wes. Don't fret another moment about it."

"I wanted you to be here for the dress," Summer says to me. She means the pictures. There are always pictures of the best friend buttoning one of a thousand buttons on the back of the dress. Summer's dress has twenty.

"I'm the right one for the job, bestie. Give me fifteen minutes and I'll be back."

"I'm timing it," Summer says.

I take a mimosa from the the table and salute her.

"Ba bo," January tells me, waving her pudgy hand in the air.

"Be right back."

I'd better hustle.

∼

First item on my agenda: check the bars. I sip the last of the mimosa and hold the glass lightly in my hand on the way to the first one, which is in the lobby of the hotel.

I don't think Linda's a liar. I think she did, in fact, scan her eyes briefly over the bar, probably from the center, by the entrance. You can't see the whole bar from there. Most of it is tucked behind a corner. Me? I go all the way in. It's coming up on noon, and the bartender looks like he's just waking up. At least his shirt is nicely pressed.

"Something to drink?"

"I'm looking for an Army veteran." I've seen Wes in the family pictures Summer kept at our old apartment, from before he went to basic training. He wasn't at the rehearsal yesterday, or the rehearsal dinner, so we haven't officially met yet, but I bet he stands up tall. Most ex-military guys do. I've met a few of them around the city. They're *not* my type. Regardless, I mimic Wes's probably posture for the bartender. "Sandy hair. Green eyes, I think." *Not a teenager anymore*, but I don't mention that.

He takes a slow look around. "Nobody like that in here now."

I match his sarcastic tone with my best bitch smile. "I can see that. Was he in here *before*?"

"Don't know. I didn't work the night shift."

"Do you know how to make a Dandy Cocktail?"

He makes a face. "No, but—"

"You, good sir, are of no use to me." I turn on one heel and stride toward the door. I can't waste any more time on this man. But I do pause before I'm all the way out and turn back. "Now, anyway. I'll probably need several drinks later. I'm going to a wedding."

He cracks a confused smile. "Okay. I won't be here by then. I'm—"

"Warn your replacement."

Next stop: the bars on the block. No time for a coat. Not that I really need one. It's the first truly warm day in April and the sun falls lightly on my shoulders as I step outside the hotel. There's one bar next door, and two across the street.

The one next door has two tourists in it who look like they haven't slept. One of them across the street doesn't open until three. And the third...

"Wes?" I call his name as soon as I'm inside. I have to hurry this up. My gorgeous best friend Summer is standing in the bridal suite right now in her bridal yoga getup, waiting for me to begin the donning of the dress.

"I'm Freddie," says the guy behind the bar. He looks me up and down. "I can be who you're looking for."

I snap my fingers and point at him. "Maybe later."

Maybe never.

I rush back into the hotel. Time is running out. Where the hell is Wes? Not in the lobby. Not in the bars. Not anywhere.

His mother gave me his room number. 331. But she said that Dayton went up there and he wasn't there.

Dayton.

I give a heavy sigh and race for the elevator.

Dayton—sexy, muscled, one-leg-and-you'd-never-know-it Dayton—is the weak link in this scenario. He probably didn't bang on the door long enough. With some men, you have to be persistent.

There's an eerie silence on the third floor; my heels are muffled by the carpet. Good. He won't hear me coming.

336. 333. 331.

I pause outside the door and listen.

No sound.

Maybe he's really not in here. What am I supposed to tell Linda? What am I supposed to tell *Summer*? Is there a jewelry store down the block where I could pick up some hasty wedding bands? That would soften the blow, I imagine.

I raise my hand to the door and pause.

Here goes nothing.

I rap confidently on the door with my knuckles, as if I'm definitely not starting to worry that Wes is well and truly gone, perhaps even out of the city. "Room service," I call out in my sexiest voice.

A moment of silence.

Then—

A soft shuffling from inside the room.

The door cracks open, and in the light from the hallway, I see the man who must be Wes.

Holy *shit*, he's hot.

The pictures of him don't do justice to the hard curve of his jaw. To the electric green eyes shot through with honey. To the shirtless, muscled body—

Shirtless? Yes, shirtless. He's got jeans on and nothing else.

"You're not room service," he says, and his voice resonates with something at the back of my spine, at the base of my core, something hot and reckless.

"I'm here to forcibly take you to a wedding," I tell him.

"Good luck with that."

He puts his hand on the door and shuts it in my face.

2

WES

I SHUT the door in her face, and she doesn't take five seconds to rebound.

I'd be impressed if I wasn't so pissed.

No hesitation. She knocks again as soon as it's shut. "I don't need luck," she calls through the door, and then it swings open. Damn it. The lock didn't engage.

Summer's best friend strides into the room like I've been playing with her. I stop in front of the television, next to the aisle between the double beds, and face her. If she wants to do this, we can do this, but I'm not going to the wedding.

I'm not.

I haven't slept. My neck aches. I push at it with my fingertips, trying to flatten the ache into submission, but it doesn't respond.

After Day's bachelor party, the cab taking us back to the hotel was in a fender-bender and I lost my fucking mind. Lost it.

Silently.

I wasn't interested in letting it show and ruining my best friend's bachelor party. It was supposed to pass, supposed to be over by the time we got out of the cab.

It wasn't over.

It's bullshit in a way that makes all other bullshit pale in comparison. I shouldn't be *affected* like this. For one thing, I'm not a fucking weakling. For another, it was Dayton who got his leg blown off in Afghanistan, not me. I came away from the Humvee with cuts and bruises.

Whitney—I know her name is Whitney, but if anybody asked me her last name, I'd be fucked—assesses me, her dark eyes flicking down to my bare feet and back to my face. "You're not dressed. I'm Whitney, by the way."

"I know who you are. I'm not going."

She cocks her head to the side and ignores my statement entirely. The sharp tone is lost on her. "Is your outfit in the garment bag or did you hang it in the bathroom?"

"You must not have heard me."

Whitney cranes her neck, then points two fingers—very sensitive of her—to the black garment bag hanging in the closet and the bathroom door. "Bag or bathroom?"

It was a fender-bender. The worst part about it was the noise, the crush of metal on metal. Both the bumpers survived, as far as I know, but the sound triggered the one memory I struggle to forget every waking moment. I've been doing a good job of forgetting the day the Humvee I was driving hit an IED on the side of the road in Afghanistan.

Dayton lost part of his leg, and I lost the part of my brain that believes the world's not out to get me.

I'm not some sort of paranoid freak. I should be past that. I was in the Army. I went back to Afghanistan after that happened, and nothing came close. On the base, I could keep it at arm's length. On the base, I didn't have to think about what I did, or where I was going to go. The powers-that-be in the Army had my name on a list, and I went where that list told me to go. That was it.

I'm not going to the wedding.

"It doesn't matter," I tell her. "I'm not getting dressed. I'm not going to the wedding. Give my apologies to Summer."

Whitney fixes me with a glare, her dark eyes narrow and sharp. Even making that face, she's pretty.

She's a little more than pretty.

She's been dolled up for the wedding. Her makeup is flawless. Her dark hair has been sleekly pulled back and twisted into some kind of arrangement at the back of her head. Summer picked sage green dresses, and against her creamy skin, the fabric is shimmering and soft.

None of that matters at all.

"That's not going to happen." She squares her shoulders. "I'm already here because your mother didn't want to commence the search by herself, and as maid of honor, it's my duty to do whatever I can to make this day absolutely magical for my best friend." She recites this like she's reading it off a contract. "However, I am not going to apologize on your behalf. That's fucking cowardly."

Shock ricochets through me. All I can do is blink at her. Nobody *ever* calls me cowardly. I'm a war hero. I've been deployed to Afghanistan more times than some people have been to an airport. Blood rushes to my face, and my whole head heats up with an instant, undeniable anger. Fuck. I'm becoming my father.

"I'm not a coward."

"I didn't say you were a coward." Whitney's voice is level as she turns to the garment bag and unzips it with a precise flick of her wrist. It's empty. The suit is out. "Ah. So you *were* planning to go."

"I wasn't—"

She marches into the bathroom, where my tuxedo hangs from the shower rod. I didn't put it there. Dayton did. He came in laughing on the day of his bachelor party and took it out of the bag. We both looked at it hanging there. "We're going to look slick as fuck," he'd said.

That was before the taxi ride.

It shouldn't be this much of a disruption. I should have been able to sleep that night—or early that morning, when I finally got back to the room and locked the door, testing it three times before I turned away. I couldn't fucking sleep. I couldn't get my eyes to shut. All the booze must have mixed with the nightmares hidden in my brain, and it put me on high alert.

High alert, looking for nothing. Nobody came to the door. Nobody shot a gun in the street. Nothing blew up. And still, it was after ten in the morning by the time my hands stopped shaking. By the time my brain ceased rocketing back to Afghanistan, to the crunch of metal at the very beginning of it all, when the shrapnel from the bomb made contact with the bottom of the Humvee. It tore through the whole fucking thing, but that sound—that sound ended everything. It ended life as I knew it, and I never saw it coming.

I should have seen it coming.

Whitney comes out of the bathroom with the tuxedo and accoutrements draped over her arm. "Undershirt first." She tosses the shirt to me, and I put it on. It seems like the right thing to do. "I don't want to hear any excuses. I'm running *very* short on time. Summer's dress isn't on."

This last bit sounds nonsensical, and a dull pain throbs at my temples. This whole event is fucked. I didn't even make the rehearsal dinner. Or the rehearsal. Shame boils in the pit of my gut. I couldn't force myself into it. The sound from the car was still ringing in my ears.

"That's too bad." I don't know if that's the right answer or not. "She'll have to put it on without me."

"You?" Whitney scoffs. "She doesn't care about *you*. She's not going to put it on without *me*. Come on. I've got your pants." She lays out the rest of the items on the bed. The cuff links. The coat. The shirt. There are fucking suspenders. What *is* this?

"You don't put the pants on first."

"Right. Sorry. My mind is addled because I had to look in *three different bars* before I realized that Dayton is an idiot. He's adorable, but he's an idiot."

"He's not an idiot."

"He didn't break the door down and haul you out. That makes him a little bit of an idiot in my book."

"That's my best friend you're talking about."

"That's your best friend you're standing up." Whitney looks baffled, and she casts a glance into the corner of the hotel room, like she's doing a reaction shot on *The Office*. "You can't let him down like this. There's nobody else who's going to do the job for you."

She tosses me the shirt and I catch it.

"Nice reflexes."

"I'm not putting this on." Sweat beads at the small of my back. I don't know how I'm going to leave the fucking hotel, much less attend the wedding. A lot could happen between the room and the reception hall, and I have no way to control it. I have no way to wrap my hands around the choking dread that's squeezing my airway.

"I did not anticipate having to dress a grown man, but"— Whitney purses her lips and comes toward me. She whips the shirt out of my hand and her fingers fly down over the button—"needs must."

Needs must? Where the hell did she learn an expression like that? I'm not sure, but up close, all I can see is the delicate pink of her lips, the cheekbone beneath the shimmering blush, and when I breathe in—holy Jesus. In her high heels, our eyes are almost at the same level...but not quite. Her eyelashes are full and beautiful against her cheeks.

Then she looks up at me.

It's a sudden move, the thing she does with her arms. The shirt flies around me, her hands come toward me, and I react. It's a gut-level reaction, not one that I can stop, and before the shirt has met my shoulders, I have her wrists in my hands.

The adrenaline surges through my veins, cold under the heat of my irritation. Every muscle flexes, ready to defend. I take one breath in—there's her scent again—and let it out. Dust motes in the air between us catch the light, and so do her dark eyes, streaked with a honey-gold that would take my breath away, if every part of me wasn't focused on survival. Her mouth rounds in shock—those pretty, pink lips—and her eyebrows move upward toward the perfect line of her hair.

We're frozen.

My heartbeat is loud in my ears. *Thud. Thud. Thud.*

On the fourth heartbeat, Whitney wriggles in my grasp. Her skin is soft, so soft, under my palms, her pulse pumping under the delicate flesh of her wrist. "Okay," she says, her voice soft but direct. "*You* can put the shirt on, if it means that much to you."

I drop her wrists and turn away.

Jesus Christ.

What the hell *was* that?

"Go," I tell her, raw command behind the word. "Get out of here. Tell Summer I'm sorry."

A pause.

"I'm not going to do that."

I round on her, voice rising. "Then *go*. I don't want you in here. I'm not going to the fucking wedding." I'm still on that adrenaline high. I take two steps toward her, blood surging in my veins, and jab a finger in her direction. "Do you even know what could *happen* between here and that fucking reception hall?"

I've lost control.

I've lost control, and now she can see it—my naked, shameful dread.

Whitney blinks. "We could stop for a drink."

"What?"

"There's a bar between here and there. I know. I looked in there for you before I came up here."

It subsides. The terror at the core of me subsides. How is she being so reasonable? How is she not running for the door?

The shirt dangles from her fingertips and she lifts it back up, holding it in front of her by the shoulders. "Shirt," she says, "then drink."

"*No!*" I thunder, and take a step closer. I'll crowd her the hell out of here if that's what I have to do. It's not what I want to do, but this—this is too much. "No."

"You need to get out of your own head," she spits, and the assessment is so piercing that it cuts me to the the quick. "I don't know what the hell you're obsessing about, but it is your *sister's wedding day,* and you are *going.* You're going, Wes. I don't really give a shit if you don't want to." She raises her fist, high color in her cheeks, and presses her knuckles into my chest. "Put your shirt on, or I'll do it for you."

The pressure on my chest is like a firecracker, a *zing* that goes all the way down to my cock. I'm so fucking pissed at her. She's so fucking pretty.

"Don't touch me," I growl.

"Then grow up and do it yourself."

"Get out of here."

"I'll get out when you're dressed."

"That doesn't make any sense."

"Nothing makes any *sense*, Wes, but you look like a fucking crazy person. Snap out of it. What do I have to do to get you to snap out of it?" Urgency makes her louder, *louder*.

"There's nothing you can do, you stupid little—"

"Don't even *go* there, asshole."

"Oh, that's lovely," I sneer, any semblance of restraint gone. "That's a lovely mouth you've got on you. Do you kiss your mother with that—"

"For the love of Christ," she says, fire in her eyes, that mouth inches from mine. "I was serious. What the hell do I have to do? We have four minutes. *Four minutes*, Wes, and I have to be back in that room. Are you going to ruin this for everyone? Are you?"

"I have other priorities."

"Get over them, or I'll—" Her eyes shine. Has she been *drinking*? They sent some almost-drunk beautiful girl to drag me to the wedding? Jesus. "I'll be forced to take drastic measures."

Another wave of rage. "Yeah?" My voice drips with contempt. "Like what?"

Whitney throws her arms around my neck and kisses me.

3

How many mimosas is *too* many before a wedding?

Turns out, four.

Wes tastes like toothpaste and heat. His body tenses—Surprise? Shock?—but it takes him less than a heartbeat to kiss me back. I have my arms around his neck, a loose hold that he could easily break away from, but he doesn't. His hands go around my waist, the white dress shirt falls to the floor, and instead of pushing me in the opposite direction, he pulls me close, my hips against his.

Why did I make him put on that undershirt? I'd do anything to run my hands down his bare abs right now.

The kiss is hard, forceful. Wes is not my type. He's the kind of guy I can't stand. But this kiss? This growling, possessive kiss? I could be into this. A shiver of sheer delight runs down my spine, and it's not because I'm in love with Wes. Jesus, no. It's because this is so *wrong*. I shouldn't be kissing Summer's brother. She is my best friend in the world.

But she wanted me to get him to the wedding at any cost, and he wouldn't shut that mouth of his. He was going to keep arguing and arguing until something drastic happened.

I'm something drastic.

He moves one of his hands and cups the back of my neck, his calloused skin rough against the wispy hairs underneath the wedding-grade updo. Hot damn. Hot *damn*. Wes might be acting like a delicate flower—a petulant, delicate flower —but he doesn't kiss like one. His tongue teases at my lips and I give into it, letting him explore for a moment before I push back, nipping at his bottom lip. He lets out a short breath and we collide, one more time, before he pushes away from me, the air electric around us.

Wes wipes the pad of his thumb against his lips, his green eyes stormy, but he doesn't turn away. He looks right into my eyes. "What the hell was that?"

"You wouldn't shut your mouth and follow the plan. Drastic measures. I think that worked to reset the conversation, don't you?" He doesn't answer while I bend to pick up the shirt from the floor. I sincerely hope he can't see the way my knees are trembling beneath the skirt of my dress. I kissed *him*. I'm the one who went there, but my body is reacting like he swept me off my feet and dropped me onto the saddle of an elegant white stallion. Ride off into the sunset with Wes? Not likely. "Put this on."

He steps close, eyes flashing.

I hold my breath, bracing for the argument, the dismissal I'll have to take back to Summer. And, oh, God, Linda.

Wes snatches the shirt from my hand. "Fine."

I exhale.

"Are you going to stand there and watch me?"

"I'm not leaving, if that's what you're asking. We're late." He buttons up the shirt and I toss him his pants. "Faster than that, oh best man."

He glances up at me, his hands on the waistband of his jeans. "You're incredibly fucking pushy."

"It gets results."

He smirks, but he gets himself into the tuxedo pants nonetheless.

"You're a lifesaver," Summer whispers. I have something like thirty seconds before I walk down the aisle. Wes is at the front with Dayton. Thank God I don't have to walk with him right now. I'll get myself together during the ceremony, and the walk out will be fine.

Summer's hands tremble around her bouquet, which is just this side of massive. It's a riot of spring roses and it's almost as beautiful as she is. "Are you all right? Do you need a tissue?" I have an entire bridal emergency kit strategically folded into my own bouquet.

"I have tissues too," whispers Alex. It's her turn after me, and then the main event.

"I'm okay," she whispers, eyes shining. "How'd you get Wes down here on time for the pictures?"

"I worked a small miracle." I give her an encouraging smile. We do *not* need to talk about the details of the miracle. All that matters, is that I got to the room in time to slide into some photos of buttoning Summer's dress—a lace confection that reminds me of Princess Kate's wedding dress, it's that classy and wonderful—and Wes was in the photos with Dayton and his other groomsman. It's some guy named Curtis. I'm more than a little desperate to know where Dayton found a guy like Curtis. The guy looks good—in his tux, he's a regular...you know, groomsman—but there's something in his eyes that makes me wonder what his story is.

"I couldn't have pulled this off without you." Summer, ever the nice one, looks at Alex. "You, either. All those doughnuts."

I take Summer's hand and squeeze, and Alex reaches out to pat her arm. "That's what best friends are for."

"I can't believe you're still mine, after I abandoned you to that apartment all by yourself."

"Solo living is a blessing, not a curse."

She cocks her head to the side, looking like a magazine ad for the expression *don't lie to me*. "Solo *rent* is a curse."

"I've got a sublease going on."

"Got or had?"

I sigh. "Had. But she took a job in LA. It's not a big deal. I'll line something up soon." The wedding coordinator hisses my name from her spot by the doorway. "It's your wedding day. Stop fretting about the apartment! Also, you look like a glorious wedding angel and I love you."

"You guys are hilarious," whispers Alex, then turns to Summer. "Why didn't you tell me she was so great? Never mind, never mind, wedding day."

Summer beams at me, and it's my turn to walk down the aisle.

Slow, measured steps. That's what we practiced at the rehearsal. Gentle smile, not a fucking terrifying grin. Shoulders down, chin slightly forward. Summer's wedding coordinator is kind of bitchy, but she does know how to get the best out of the wedding photos. I can respect that.

I focus on the gentle smile and not on Wes.

I'm *totally* not looking at him, standing there in his tux, a step away from Dayton, posture tall and precise, like I thought it would be. I am not noticing his sandy hair, a couple of shades darker than Summer's, or the way he flicks his eyes to me as I come down the aisle. I don't even *see* how his eyes heat up at the sight of me. Gentle smile. Gentle smile. *Do not* get turned on by the memory of his lips on mine while I'm walking down the aisle at my best friend's wedding.

I feel it before it happens—the damn aisle runner. There's a crease and it catches the toe of my high heel. No. *No.* But I am a photogenic goddess in this moment and I will not be thwarted by an aisle runner. I will not have Wes see me fall on my face in front of the church.

I lift my heel high—too high—and pray nobody's taking a picture. A couple of little gasps rise in the air around me, but I save it. By God, I save it. I put my foot firmly back down on the ground and take the next step.

Don't look at him. Don't look at him. Shoulders down, chin out—

Fuck. I looked.

He's smirking again, that asshole.

Smirking like *I'm* the hilarious joke at this wedding and not the best man who almost didn't show up. My cheeks burn, but I keep my gentle smile on like a true professional. Shoulders down, chin slightly forward.

I climb the steps, onto the dais, with no further incident and take my place on the other side of the officiant, who is a woman from the Unitarian Church with curly hair that is *to die for*. It spills down her back, reddish and shining. Maybe *she* can be my new best friend, now that Summer moved out.

No. I'd never replace her, but the officiant—Kristi—*is* one of those people you instantly like. She's a hugger too. The thing I like best about her is that she's blocking my view of Wes.

I stand slightly on an angle as Alex comes down the aisle, slightly too fast. You can't win them all.

Then it's Summer's turn.

There's a whisper of fabric as everyone rises, a swell of music, and oh, my God, my heart aches at the perfect coordination of it all. Summer is lit by the floor-to-ceiling windows on this side of the hall, and even behind the delicate sheen of her veil, I can see how hard she's smiling. Her eyes shine with tears. She and her dad pause inside the door for the photographer, and she looks up at him as if for reassurance. He looks down at her, pride illuminating his face.

It's a moment I will never, ever experience. I lower my lashes and look at the floor.

Then the music rises again, and Summer's dad walks her down the aisle. I pick up my head—shoulders down, chin slightly out—because the photographers are going to get a shot of Summer from the back as she comes toward her fiancé.

She can't take her eyes off him. Halfway down the aisle, she mouths the word, *You*. Dayton says it back, then puts a fist to his mouth. Jesus, this is going to be a sob-fest if people don't get it together. Starting with me.

I take a deep breath and let it out. Summer arrives at the stairs and her dad walks her up, and then there's a whole process involving Dayton shaking his hand and taking his bride by the arm. The officiant launches into a speech about two people coming together in the bond of marriage. I listen until she compares a new love to the springtime, full of hope, because for me, it's not that way, though I'd never say that to Summer. Not now. Of course not now. Not even when we're two bottles in at Vino Veritas and sharing sex secrets with each other. No way.

It's time for the vows.

It's my time to leap into action—graceful, practiced action. Summer turns and I step to her side. Her bouquet is heavy as fuck, but I wear a gentle smile nonetheless. It's a good thing I've been lifting at the gym, honestly, because my pre-weights arm muscles would give out under the combined weight of our flowers.

All four of us in the bridal party are facing the bride and groom.

I feel his eyes on me.

I keep my gaze focused on Summer's veil and do my best to listen to what they're promising.

"—support you always in following your dreams," says the officiant.

"I promise to support you always in following your dreams," says Summer, a waver in her voice. "Even if I think they're dumb."

Everyone laughs, including Dayton, and he raises a hand to wipe a tear from the corner of his eye.

My eyes slide off his face—it's so *intimate,* being this close to them, and I don't want to see him cry, for God's sake. What if he breaks down right now? It's one thing for a man to mist at his wedding, but ugly sobs? No. I'm nervous at the thought of it.

Looking away from Dayton means I'm looking right at Wes.

Has he been staring at me the whole time?

He has.

His eyes are intense, as if he's trying to figure out who the hell I am, exactly. As if he's trying to figure out whether I'm going to jump him again. I'm *not*, but he liked it before, even if he doesn't want to admit it.

I liked it before, even if I'll *never* admit it.

The officiant announces the new Mr. and Mrs. Dayton Nash and the cheers from the guests crash in around me. It's time. A jubilant Summer takes her bouquet back and they head down the aisle, Dayton's hand wrapped around hers.

Wes and I approach one another, meeting in the center of the dais, and he offers his elbow. I take it. *Zing.* My hand on his tuxedo jacket heats up. I hold my head up high and we walk down the stairs, down the aisle.

We get to the doors of the reception hall and step out into the hallway.

I turn my head to comment on a job well done.

He cuts me off.

"Whoa," he says, stepping back. "I'm going to the reception. I don't need more convincing."

My cheeks go hot. *Again.* Damn it, *why* did I enjoy that kiss so much? He's an asshole.

"Aww, that's cute," I say with a sharp snap in my voice. "But I wouldn't waste my time."

Then I lead the way into the cocktail hour.

4

THIS RECEPTION IS my idea of a nightmare.

Relatives and friends—Jesus, the friends—are crowded into the reception hall, shouting at each other at the top of their lungs. I don't know who's worse—Summer's old friends, or mine. Dayton, somehow, has kept in touch with a group from high school. The married ones look like they'd rather be anywhere else, and the single ones can't stop checking out Summer's friends.

Speaking of...

If Summer's friends screech one more time, I'll lose my mind. The high-pitched sound burrows into a part of my mind that makes me want to slip quietly out the side door and never return. What the hell could possibly be so exciting? It's a wedding, for God's sake. All of this runs on a script.

A script that I almost singlehandedly fucked up.

I take another swig of beer and swallow the shame along with it.

Summer's maid of honor had to come haul me out of a hotel room.

Christ almighty.

I saw the hurt flash though her eyes when I made that comment after the ceremony. After I made it about her lack of control over herself. I know it cut her.

You'd never know it, looking at her now.

Whitney flits from table to table, the fake candle center-pieces casting a gentle glow over the curves of her dress. It fits her like a glove, and so does the smile she's wearing. A girl from high school—I don't remember her name—says something and Whitney tips her head back and laughs. I see Summer's name on her lips, and, *So gorgeous.*

My sister does look gorgeous. She is radiant, sitting next to Day at the head table, her hand on his. I was kind of a prick to both of them. It's almost disgusting, what good people they both turned out to be. Summer always was. Day had his moments. But you'd never know I punched him in the face by how he greets me when I come to see them, and little January. *That* girl—it's embarrassing how much my niece makes me laugh. I'd rather be hanging out with her, but my mom's the lucky one in the quiet hotel room, letting her sleep.

I tighten my grip on my beer and drain the rest of it.

The worst is yet to come.

There's a crackle over the DJ system, and my gut clenches.

I know what's coming, and I don't want to do this.

"I'm pleased to announce," says the DJ, who reminds me of Peter Hollis, a guy I knew in high school, who thought he'd be a great sports commentator, but had the most obnoxious voice known to mankind, "that the bride and groom will be sharing their first dance, followed by the father-daughter dance."

We all watch Summer and Dayton sway around the dance floor, glowing in the lights from the DJ station. I tap my foot against the floor, faster and faster, until I become aware of it. I am surrounded by friends of my parents, the women sniffling into tissues at the sight.

That's never going to be me.

I rearrange my face into something closer to a pleasant, blank expression and less like a scowl as my dad cuts in, beaming at Summer. All of this is a bit much.

Unlike Summer and Day's song, which dragged on for approximately an hour, this one sounds like it's playing double-time.

There's a round of applause, as if they've done something spectacular, and then that damn DJ is on his mic again. "The bride and groom now invite the bridal party to join them on the dance floor. Let the party begin!"

Summer's other bridesmaid, Alex, and Whitney rush onto the floor and hug Summer, probably murmuring congratulations. Curtis is right behind them. For a guy who apparently had some serious issues going on earlier in the year, he looks totally at ease, one hand on Alex's waist, the other holding her hand lightly. It's so fucking *appropriate.*

I put down the beer bottle on the table and go to Whitney.

She doesn't hesitate. Not for an instant. Her left hand settles on the curve of my shoulder, her right hand slips into mine, and that smile on her face doesn't waver.

"Smile," she says through her teeth. "We're being photographed. Chin slightly out..."

"What?"

She flicks her eyes up toward the ceiling and back. Her waist feels hot to the touch, but it must be my hand. There's too little fabric between us for this to be *fine* and too much for what I want, even if I need to keep her at arm's length. "You'd know if you'd come to the rehearsal."

I have to.

She's too volatile.

"I didn't."

Whitney tips her head back and laughs, and it's the prettiest thing I've ever seen. The camera flashes. "So, what's wrong with you? Did you have a bad day? We can talk about it now, if you want. My duties are significantly less pressing now that dinner is over. This way." She sways her weight, trying to take us to the center of the crowd, but I overpower her. Subtly. It doesn't take as much as I'd thought.

Her words land.

"You want to talk about whether I had a bad *day*?" This is a bewildering development.

"Well, you've acted like a complete prick since the moment I knocked on the door." She's still smiling, radiant, and it strikes me how *good* she's going to look in the pictures. "Nobody acts like such a douchebag unless something's going on."

"I reject the stereotype." The beat of the song picks up, and I spin us both toward the edge of the dance floor. "I've met a ton of people who are pricks with no motivation."

"Oh? Which one are you, then?"

There's approximately a snowball's chance in hell that I'm going to tell her the truth. Not here. Not now. Not ever. She's never going to know about the taxi, the sound, the way that fucking Humvee haunts my waking dreams.

"These days, I'm just a regular, grade-A prick."

Whitney laughs again, more subdued this time. "That's surprising. I'd have thought you'd have balls the size of Texas, trying to skip out on your sister's wedding."

It's my turn to laugh, and I don't see it coming. "You're something else."

The song changes, to some loud-ass crowd pleaser, and Whitney pulls away. "You don't know the half of it."

∼

Two Weeks Later

I'm MID-SQUAT, two-twenty-five on the bar, when my phone rings on the mat.

I cut one glance down at it. It's a number from the city.

I get in one more rep, the phone still ringing, put the bar into the rack, and snatch the phone up.

"Wes Sullivan."

"Mr. Sullivan, my name is Sheila, and I'm calling on behalf of Gregory Miller in the surveillance unit here at Visionary Response."

"Okay." Very fucking smooth. "I'm—" I'm at the gym, still breathing hard, and the name *Visionary Response* blends in with twenty other company names. I've been applying for a *lot* of jobs. There are never any surprises on the application forms. Name, date, experience. I have plenty of that, and with military acronyms, it sounds a thousand times more impressive. "I'm listening."

God.

"Mr. Miller would like to extend you an offer for the project manager position you applied for. Congratulations!"

"Thank you." Sheila must've seen my resume. Better to fall back on a clipped military demeanor than come off like a total jackass in this moment.

"Would you mind holding for a brief moment?"

"Yes, I can—" Before I finish my sentence, there's a *click* and hold music plays, a jazzy rendition of some Top Forty bull-shit. "Okay."

"Mr. Sullivan," the voice booms from the other end of the line, and I jerk the phone away from my ear. Christ, he's loud. "This is Greg Miller, head of surveillance at Visionary. Seven years in the armed forces, yes?"

He's seen my resume, right? "Yes, that's...accurate."

"Thank you for your service. Let me just start by saying that. Thank you for your service to our country."

I never know what the fuck to say when people say this to me. If it's in person, which it usually is, I nod. It's not like I can shout, "You're welcome" at them. It's not like I'm a hero. I did a job. It was a dangerous one. Maybe I was a hero then, but not anymore.

Conveniently, Greg Miller barrels on, not waiting for me to acknowledge his gift of thanks. "I was impressed by your resume, Wes, and I'm happy to offer you a spot on our team as project manager."

"That sounds great."

He laughs, a great big belly laugh, and I turn back toward the gym mirror. I'm not looking my best right now, what with the furrowed brow, but why the hell is he laughing.

"Sir?"

"I've never had anyone accept a position that fast."

I chuckle. It seems like the right thing to do. "I wouldn't have applied if I didn't want the job."

Never mind that this application has long since blended in with all the others. Never mind that the real reason I applied to so many places is that I *have* to get out of Newark.

"We're offering a starting salary of ninety-eight."

I blink at myself in the mirror. "Ninety-eight?"

"That's correct."

"That sounds great."

"Wes, this isn't like the Army. You're welcome to negotiate on the salary." No shit, it's not like the Army. The Army is all that's keeping the nightmares at bay, which is a fun fucking thing to find out when you've already made the transition back to civilian life.

"A hundred and ten," I say. I'm in the *gym*. I'm not prepared to negotiate, and I don't really care what the salary is. My breathing has settled but my heart pounds in my chest; a strange mix of excitement and irritation.

"One-oh-five," says Greg.

"That sounds great."

He laughs again. "I like you. We'll see you in the office at nine on Monday."

Hold on.

"Nine on Monday?" I repeat back, on the off chance that he's shitting me.

"That's correct. We need to hit the ground running. Sheila will email you a welcome packet with instructions on how to get to the office. You can sign all the paperwork first thing. Welcome to the team, Wes."

"Thanks, I—" Another click. This time, there's no hold music.

Okay, then.

I pace back and forth in front of the squat racks, swiping through my phone.

It's Friday.

The job starts Monday.

There is no *way* I'm calling Greg Miller back and asking him for more time. I need a job more than I've ever needed anything. I need a *schedule*. Maybe that will shove the night-mares into that lockbox where they should be fucking living.

I dial Summer's number.

She picks up on the first ring.

"Wes?"

She's whispering.

"Hey. Did I call at a bad time?"

"It's ten in the morning. I'm at work."

"Shit. Sorry."

There's a silence.

"Did you need something?"

"I got a job."

"Oh, my God!" She forgets that she's whispering. "Congratu-lations, Wes! Where is it?"

"At Visionary Response, in the city. I start on Monday."

"That's *so* great," she says, the warmth in her voice palpable through the phone. "Do you have a place lined up yet? Are you already here?" Excitement rises in her tone.

"I still need a place. I was hoping I could crash with you for a while."

"You know you're always welcome..."

"But?"

"But January—" I can practically see her face scrunching under the worry. "I think she's teething again, and it's awful. She wakes up screaming four times a night. It's...it's really loud." She talks faster, squeezing in more words with every breath. "I won't be offended at all if that's not the kind of place you want to spend your first... Your roommate doesn't want to move, then?"

My roommate has been gone for three months, vanished into thin air. Bennett Powell got out of the service, got drunk on freedom, and quit paying the rent a long time ago. I met him in Newark when he first got out. He sent me one text after he left—**had to hit the road, meet up later?**—and after that, I stopped looking.

That's not the most pressing issue.

I know what'll happen if a scream like that wakes me up over and over again. Summer must know that too. It makes me wonder if Day is as settled as he seems, or if she's spending her nights rushing to the baby before the sound gets to him. "It's not a big deal, Summer. I'll find a place. There have to be a million subleases available."

"You know what?" There's a clicking in the background. "I'll find one for you. I'm *really* good at this."

"You don't have to do that."

"I will. I will, Wes, and you're not going to stop me." She claps her hands, the sound echoing over the line. "I'll find the perfect place for you. You'll see."

"BUT IF I DIE, I won't need life insurance."

I tilt my head and give Hollywood's Man of the Year a welcoming grin, as if it's him on the other end of the line and not Bill, from an educationally lacking town called Lakeview. Not the real Man of the Year, obviously, but a photo of him I tore from a magazine. It helps me visualize that I'm talking to someone sensual and attractive. Constant acting practice. Constant.

"Mr. Jenkins—may I call you Mr. Jenkins? The life insurance policies we offer at American Blue aren't meant to cover your personal expenses. They're meant to assist your family, should you pass away unexpectedly."

"Oh, shit," he says. "I thought it was, like, for cars."

"A similarly named product, but it serves a very different purpose."

"Do you sell health insurance then?"

"We don't."

"Then what *do* you sell?"

Another winning smile goes to the Hollywood Man of the Year. "We can offer homeowners insurance, automobile insurance, life insurance, and rental insurance. Are you in need of any of those?"

"I don't have any kids."

"Do you have a home?"

This is hopeless.

"I don't need any insurance."

I launch into the part of my script that comes with as much relief as a full-body massage. "Nonetheless, thank you for giving me the opportunity to talk to you about the services we offer. If there's anything else we at American Blue can do for—"

There's a *click*. Bill Jenkins hung up on me.

I lean back in my chair and rub at my eyes. Last night was not an ideal night for waking up rested. I've had callbacks for two auditions, and I'm waiting to hear from Christy, my agent, about whether I was hired for any jobs. Either one would make it a lot easier to pay the rent. I've got savings, but this is New York City—they're not enough to float me for long.

My cell phone vibrates in my purse, which is tucked into the bottom drawer of my desk. I sit upright in a hurry, but I keep it graceful. Every moment is an opportunity to practice being a movie star, so I wink at Hollywood Man of the Year and reach in a *very* refined manner to open the drawer and lift my phone from my purse.

It's Christy.

"Christy, how are you?" I answer, like I know she's calling with good news.

"Whit, I've got some bad news."

Great.

"You didn't make final callbacks for the commercial or the pilot."

Double great.

"But we'll keep trying." Her voice rises with enthusiasm. For an agent, she's a damn good actress. "I've got a couple other possibilities in the wings."

Christy *always* has possibilities in the wings. Not many of them turn out to be real jobs.

My heart sinks deeper into my toes but I give the Man of the Year a cheeky wink. "I'm looking forward to it!"

"Talk soon!"

This is not good.

I wasn't exactly truthful with Summer when she asked me about roommates at her wedding. The truth is, I've had six different roommates since she left. All of them sucked in various different ways. One was perfectly nice, but only needed the room for a month, since she was off to join the Peace Corps. One was a guy who I'm *pretty* sure was dealing drugs, but he was quiet and neat. I was almost sad when he left after six weeks, pressing the rest of the month's rent into my hand.

But the last one?

He was a grade-A creep. I felt like I was living in a psychological thriller. There would be a noise in the night, a creak of the floorboard, and I *felt* a presence outside my bedroom door. You can bet your ass I deadbolted that thing every night. I learned how to install a deadbolt too. That took exactly forty-eight hours and thirteen different YouTube videos.

He was normal during the daytime, which was why it was *so* weird. But once I went to the bathroom in the night and found him standing in the doorway of his bedroom door, motionless. I wouldn't have seen him if the light from the bathroom hadn't illuminated his face at the last moment.

It's honestly shocking that I didn't die of a massive heart attack, I was so fucking scared.

Bottom line: I don't have a roommate. I kicked him out after a month, brandishing the short-term lease contract we'd both signed, and since then, I haven't been able to search.

The only problem?

New York City is expensive as hell. I'm an aspiring actress; not Meryl Streep, though, so my savings aren't limitless. I could afford a couple of months of solo living while I honed my self-defense skills, but not much longer.

I purse my lips and consider my desk phone. I should be making another cold call—that *is* most of my job—but I need a minute. I smile, huge, as if I'm thrilled with the news, *rapturous* at the news. "Opportunities in the wings," I say out loud.

Faking it until I make it is not working in this moment of my life.

My phone vibrates in my hand.

It's a text from an unknown number, piquing my interest.

I sit up straight in my chair and bend my head studiously toward the screen so that it looks like I'm working, and open the message.

Unknown: Is this still Whitney?

I type out **No, this is a phone** and snicker to myself, my hard-won good mood making a swift comeback. Who could this be? Anyone who *really* knows me knows that I wouldn't give up my phone number for anything. You'd have to pry that number from the cold, dead wreckage of my cell phone company. Not a chance. *People* have that number. At least one casting director, and up to ten. They could wake up in the middle of the night and realize I'm their girl for the breakout hit of the season. I wouldn't risk that on *changing my number.*

Whitney: Yeah. Who's this?

Unknown: Oh cool! I didn't think it would still be your number, since it's been so long!

Unknown: This is Eva Lipton! It's Eva!

I can't tell if I feel queasy or excited at the sight of the name.

Nope, it's definitely queasy.

Why, after all these years, is she texting me out of the blue like this?

Why are you texting me out of the blue like this? I type it out and delete it. Shit. She's probably seen that I was responding. I need to say *something*. And yet...how dare she

force me to respond like this? I don't care that she's seen that
... indicator in our conversation. If she's staring at her phone
like I am, that is.

**Whitney: Eva! Wow! It's been forever! I can't believe you
still have my number!**

**Eva: Are you kidding? I remember our first cell phones.
There's no way I'd ever delete it. It's been, what, twelve
phones by now?**

Whitney: At least. So—what's up?

It's not that I *want* to rush her through the conversation, but
I don't have unlimited time to text at my desk before it
becomes, in my supervisor Howard's words, *a bit of a
problem.*

**Eva: I moved to New York! I'm living in Astoria. Meet up
with me! I want to know all about your glamorous life as
an actress!**

MY STOMACH CURDLES. *Yes, it's so glamorous, fielding rejection
calls from an agent who's somehow an even more chipper person
than you are.* That's not even the worst of it. The worst of it is
that Eva actually *is* a success in her chosen field.

I'm not jealous. I don't subscribe to the idea of coveting the
things other people have, because you never know what's
lurking behind that happiness. Still, I did feel a pang of
envy...no, *admiration*...when Eva's debut novel hit all the
bestseller lists over the winter. It's one of those thrillers, one
of those books everybody's talking about. She got a movie

deal. *I* can't get a movie deal, and she got one writing a book.

"Comparison is the thief of joy," I say out loud to Hollywood's Man of the Year. There's no reason not to meet up with Eva, if I'm being honest about it. She's always been kind to me, even if she wasn't nice. And we're all grown up now. I know as well as anyone that you should cherish your old friends while you try your damndest to make new ones.

I sigh, then give Hollywood's Man of the Year a thumbs-up to get in the mood.

WHITNEY: We absolutely have to! Where and when?

IT'LL BE FUN, I tell myself. It'll be a nice distraction from all this crap. I can wow her with some audition nightmares, things like that, and she'll be impressed that I keep going back. Not that I need her approval...but it would be nice.

I'm half-hoping she'll be vague about the details.

She isn't.

EVA: Not this weekend but next? I've got to finish some moving stuff but then I'll be free.

WHITNEY: Anywhere you'd like to go?

EVA: Your favorite place. :)

God, she out-sweets the best of them.

I hesitate over the phone. I know where my favorite place is, but it seems almost like a betrayal to invite her there instead of Summer.

Which is stupid.

I can invite Summer anytime. She has a husband and a baby, not a prison sentence, and she is still my best friend.

WHITNEY: **Vino Veritas, by my place. You need directions?**

EVA: **I'll Google. 7:00? Saturday?**

WHITNEY: **Sounds perfect!**

EVA: **:D**

THAT'S THAT, then.

Time for me to get back to my job, connecting people with the insurance policies they need to live their best lives.

I'm bent over the open desk drawer, about to drop the phone from my fingertips into the dark confines of my purse, when it rings in my hand. I can't take another call from Christy right now. I drop it in, and it lands face-up.

It's not Christy, it's Summer.

"Hey," I say quickly into the phone. "I'm at work."

"Sorry sorry sorry," she says, breathing hard like she's walking fast to meet a train. "I'm on my way to a meeting at the VA so I only have, like, five seconds. Can I ask you a question?"

"I think you just did."

She laughs out loud. "Seriously!"

"Seriously, ask me a question. Get me fired. I can't believe you're going to end my career this way, but in light of our relationship, I have no choice but to—"

"Are you at your *desk*?"

"Yes! Didn't you hear me when I said I was at work?"

"I thought you meant you were in the breakroom or something."

"That would be more awkward than talking about this at my desk."

"Hey, how are things going?" Genuine concern fills Summer's voice and spills out through the phone. It makes my heart warm, but it also uncovers the sting of rejection. Ouch. "I've missed you, since I moved out. We should go to Vino soon."

"This weekend?"

"Yes. Day can stay with January on Saturday afternoon. But you *cannot* send me home plastered. It's not a good look on a doting mother."

"Yuck. Don't say *doting*."

"Sorry," she says, laughing again. Summer has a kind laugh. I wonder if I'd sound like that if everything were lined up in neat little rows in my life. Not that her life is like that. She didn't expect to get pregnant with Dayton, but she's slipped into the role as effortlessly as a lubed-up dick into a willing orifice. "But, Whit—"

"Tell me. What is it? Your wish is my command."

"You are so weird."

"Same to you, sister."

"Okay. I'm at the building. Are you ready to hear what I have to say?"

"I'm all ears."

"I need to ask you a favor." Summer hesitates. "A big favor."

6

"You've had a lot of bad ideas in your life, Sunny, but this one's the worst."

"I disagree," Summer says. "It's the perfect solution. She needs a roommate. You need a room."

Two of those things are true. I do need a room. Commuting from Newark is soul-crushingly obnoxious, and I have no reason to live there anymore. It was a pipe dream I followed after leaving Fort Drum, and like all pipe dreams, it didn't pan out. And Whitney probably does need a roommate.

But it's not the perfect solution.

I'm only going along with it because what the hell else am I going to do? I've visited three other places this week, and all of them set me the fuck off. Is everyone in the city a drug-addicted slob? So much for finding something decent within my price range.

This is the last option. That doesn't mean it's a good one.

"She's really a great person," Summer says. "You met her at the wedding, so you already know that."

I know more than Summer thinks. "Yes. I met her before the wedding. You sent her after me like a fucking attack dog."

Sunny laughs. "She's not an attack dog. She can be a little...intense, but she's almost always happy. You'll like her if you get to know her."

Getting to know her isn't the issue. She's not the kind of person I need in my life. She's too flighty, too in-your-face, too unpredictable. No fucking way.

But being that close?

Jesus.

It's been two weeks since the wedding, and I can still taste her on my lips. I can still feel the electric jolt in my palms when I took her waist in my hands, feel the curve of her hips under the fabric of that dress. My cock jumps at the memory. God. Think about anything else. Think about wet newspapers. Think about the desert sand in my mouth. Think about...don't think about that.

"I can tell you're stewing about this," Summer says into the silence over the phone. "You really shouldn't, Wes. It's a great apartment. It's a great location. So close to your job. And she works a lot. She won't be a bother."

"She's being a real pain in the ass right now," I shoot back. "This meeting is ridiculous." A curl of irritation winds its way up through my chest and squeezes at my heart, threatening to harden into rage. I shouldn't have to be at her beck and call to get a fucking sublease.

"She has a good heart," Summer says gently. "Indulge her. I promise, it'll be worth it."

Goose bumps rise on the back of my neck, and I put my hand up to cover them. It sounds like she's talking about being with Whitney, not just sharing an apartment. She's not, but her words hum with a double meaning that makes me suspicious.

"What do you mean, it'll be worth it?"

There's a muffled noise on the other end of the line—Summer covering her phone with her hand. Then—"Wes? Are you still there?"

"Yeah."

"Sorry. January woke up from her nap and she needs me. The meeting will be fine. You're going to love her. I gotta go! Bye!"

You're going to love her.

I slip my phone back into my pocket and scan the block ahead for the place we're supposed to meet.

There it is—the sign. A trendy neon thing on a black back-board, the light shaped like a wine glass.

My soul recoils.

If she thinks she's going to get the upper hand, she's dead wrong.

~

"WE'RE NOT MEETING HERE."

Whitney blinks up at me from a table tucked along the side wall of a wine bar that's both trendy and hipster in a way that makes my skin crawl. The wait staff is uniformly willowy, even the guys, and I'm not going to sit here, sipping wine out of an oversized glass just to appease her.

"We're already here."

"No. Hard pass."

She narrows her eyes. "You're supposed to be wooing me, so you won't be homeless when you start your new job."

"You're supposed to be impressing *me*, so you won't be homeless when I start my new job."

Whitney purses her lips into a red lipstick pouting grin. "I'm not nearly that destitute."

"I know how rent is in the city." If I didn't, I wouldn't be meeting her here, in this wine bar, for any length of time.

"I know how men are in the city. What's the problem with meeting here?"

I glance around. Is she seeing what I'm seeing? Is she seeing me standing here, looking like a fucking asshole? "It's not my kind of place."

She sighs, lowering her glass to the table. "What is your kind of place?"

"I'll show you."

"But I—" Whitney huffs a breath out through her nose. "Fine." She lifts the glass to her lips and tosses the rest of it back in one go. It's not half a minute before she's tossed a twenty on the table, gathered her purse, and followed me out.

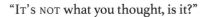

"It's NOT what you thought, is it?"

Whitney looks around Macmillan's, suspicion shining in her eyes. "No."

"Why is your face like that?"

"Because, Wes Sullivan, I can't tell if you brought me here to fuck with me, or because this is actually your bar."

"Wes, sit down. You're making everybody nervous," calls the bartender, Keith, while he slides two beers to a couple on high stools.

Whitney smiles and gives Keith a little wave. Even from all the way over here by the door, I can see the burly man's cheeks go a ruddier shade. "So, it *is* your bar," she says to me.

"What did you expect?"

"I expected a *dive*." She looks skyward, as if picturing the scene. "Something manly. Something rough. I don't know. Biker guys around a pool table."

I look sidelong at her. "You think I hang around in places like *Road House*?" I mean the *Road House before* Swayze shows up. Jesus.

Whitney does that little closed-mouth grin again, and it's cute. Not that I'm ever going to tell her that. "You have some...rough aspects to your personality. By which I mean that sometimes you act like a total asshole."

I laugh. "You've got it all wrong. Assholes are too good for dive bars."

"Not the ones I've met."

"Maybe you haven't met the right one."

Whitney chuckles, and her gaze flicks to the floor. What *was* that? All I did was make a joke about meeting the right asshole, and the confident, take-no-prisoners persona fell away. My heart picks up. Maybe there's more to her than that.

Not that it matters. I'm never going to be with a girl like her.

"Let's grab a table." I head for my favorite spot in the back corner and slide into the booth, my back against the wall, full view of the restaurant. The only thing I can't see is the kitchen, but the door to the back is three feet away, and it's as tiny as they come, so if anybody makes trouble, I'll be the first to know, after the cooks.

"Nice table." Whitney tucks her purse in next to her and grabs one of the laminated menus from a holder on the wall. "You can buy me an apology dinner."

"An apology dinner?"

That smile. "I think we got off on the wrong foot."

I lean back and cross my arms over my chest. "You came on a little strong."

"Because you—" She drops the menu and raises both hands into the air. "Let's not play the blame game, even if it *is* your fault that I had to go on a *Mission: Impossible* search for you." She looks straight at me, eyes dark and deep. "We both need something out of this."

There it is again—that pickup in the chest, a beat of my heart that serves as a warning. There's more than one meaning layered in her words, and in the back of my mind I hear it: the question I refuse to ask. What does *she* need?

"I need an apartment."

"I need rent money." She looks down again and I see her face without any walls, completely vulnerable. It's a squeeze around my heart, that moment. I don't get it. She is *all* wrong for me. She is ridiculous and vibrant and self-centered and pushy. She's all the things I don't want in a woman. She's too *loud*. She's just too loud.

Beyond that, I know—she needs more than rent money. My heart might be overreacting, racing along inside my chest, but my gut is saying, *Back the hell up. Get away from a girl who needs more from you than rent money. You're in no position to give it.*

In the kitchen, something metal crashes to the floor, the sound reverberating out into the restaurant and through the table, through my fingertips, a *zap* straight to the heart. It was already beating fast, but now all the beats blur into one painful, powerful *thud*. I press my fingertips harder into the wood surface of the table, the knuckles going white, and fight it.

The seat underneath me lifts off the ground, the wheels losing contact with the road, and I tighten my grip instinctively on the steering wheel, though I don't know what I can do. We've been hit. We've been hit. The Humvee lurches to the right, the floor underneath me a yawning hole that I've barely missed. Dust chokes the air in here, and I'm saying something. The words don't connect from my mouth to my brain. It's all autopilot and the communication system squawks. I can't hear a fucking thing, my ears ringing, and the heat is too intense, even for the desert.

"Wes," he says, but he couldn't have said that. The explosion underneath the Humvee incapacitated him. I dragged him out myself, saw the mess of his left leg with my own eyes, the blood, the wreckage.

A hand covers mine, soft and small, and I jerk away. "Wes?"

I blink and suck in a breath. Air in the lungs. Breathe. You're not in a fucking Humvee. You're in Macmillan's, with Whitney, of all people. Her eyes are huge and dark, and she brings her hand to her chest slowly. No sudden movements.

"Yeah?"

"You okay?" Her voice comes from far off at first, then snaps back into my focus, along with the sounds from the rest of the bar. Glasses clinking against one another as Keith pulls them from underneath the counter. The soft murmur of that couple at the bar. She laughs at his joke. The front door opens, letting in a long curl of fresh spring air. Even in New York City, I can smell the trees in bloom.

"What are you talking about?" I grab a menu from the holder on the wall. "I'll buy you an apology dinner, if that's what you really want."

IT TAKES three trains to get to work from Newark, and I hate every single one of them.

Each one is more crowded by the minute. I've been leaving early, to avoid rush hour, but there's no such thing. No matter what, the train is a mess by the time I get into the city. People are too close, and inevitably there's some crazy asshole when I step off at 60th. My shoulders tense, the pain reaching a hand up to my temples and pressing in hard. By the time I get to the office, it's a matter of plastering on a half-pleasant expression and downing the coffee I couldn't hold on the train. I have to have my hands free.

Except today.

I've got all my stuff with me in two black suitcases, because after work, I'm moving in with Whitney.

Newark is a minefield in more ways than one, so after the dinner at Macmillan's, we agreed to split the rent for one month, two months maximum.

"A short-term thing," she'd said lightly.

"I want my own place."

Her shoulders had sagged a fraction of an inch, but the smile never left her face. "Of course."

Then she'd ordered a brownie to go and told them to add it to the bill.

That girl has a pair of brass ones, that's for sure.

It brings a smile to my face, thinking about that damn brownie, even while I'm dragging two suitcases from the subway to my office, head throbbing. The tension seeps out from my head to my shoulders, an iron rail I can't shake off. I ended the lease on my place in Newark over the weekend. There's no going back.

At the office, my shoulders relax. I know what's going to happen here. Same as every other day.

Visionary Response's headquarters for New York City are in a low-slung building in Midtown. We scan ID cards to go through the lobby to the elevators. I usually take the stairs, but two rolling suitcases would make that an enormous pain in the ass, so elevator it is. The wheels squeak on the polished floor. Up to the fourth floor, across a carpeted lobby, and in through a set of glass doors. Up front, we've got a hallway lined with meeting rooms, and then a big, open bullpen full of cubicles. Mine is toward the back left corner, and my boss, Greg, is striding up the aisle toward me when I get in. I'm still twenty minutes early, even with the suitcases.

"I know you love the job, Sullivan, but this is a little much." He gestures to the suitcases with his titanium all-day coffee tumbler.

I shrug my shoulders in an "Aww shucks" way. "I couldn't let you down, boss. You need me here."

He laughs and steps out of the way, so I can pull the suitcases into the cubicle. I line them up on the outer edge so they won't be in the way. "It's freakishly clean in here. Did you know that?"

I snort. "Please. I've seen your office. I know about the dust buster."

"I'm not ashamed of the dust buster. It's a Black & Decker." I pick up the pile of papers in my inbox and leaf through them. "Seriously. Are you taking a trip or something?"

"Moving into the city today."

"Commute was killing you, huh?"

He has no idea. "It's a bit far from Newark."

"Where's the new place?"

"About eight blocks."

"Army buddy?"

I almost laugh out loud but catch myself at the last moment. "No. The opposite of an Army buddy. It's actually my sister's old roommate."

Greg raises his eyebrows. "Your sister, Summer?"

"I only have one sister."

"She was living with a guy?"

My God. "No. One of her friends from college."

He doesn't understand, and then he does. "You're living with a woman?"

"I hate to break this to you, Greg, but you live with a woman too."

"She's my *wife*."

"I'm not getting married in order to sublet an apartment. Come on, Greg. I'd have invited you."

"I'm flattered." He takes a long sip of his coffee. "You don't think things will be a little...*tense*?"

"Tense? Why?" I give him a wide-eyed stare.

He takes the bait. "You, in a small apartment, with a living, breathing American woman? You're telling me that's not going to heat up?"

I think of Whitney's lips on mine, the sparkling flavor of a mimosa on her tongue, the way she moved against me like there was nothing in the world that could stop her from the kiss. And then I think of the way she looked at me at Macmillan's, that flash of vulnerability in her eyes.

"No. It's not going to heat up. It's not that kind of arrangement."

Greg raises his tumbler toward me. "Yet."

Yet is his thing. Whenever we haven't achieved something in the department, it's only a matter of time. We haven't done it *yet*. We don't have those skills *yet*.

"Never. I'm not going to go after my sister's best friend."

"A guy like you doesn't have to go after women. I'd bet my quarterly bonus on it."

"We don't have a quarterly bonus, unless you're holding out on me."

"Guess we'll find out," says Greg. Then he laughs at his own joke and leaves me to start my day.

"You didn't bring much."

Whitney eyes the suitcases as I pull them in the front door of the apartment. It's almost seven, and I can tell she's been waiting because, once again, she looks flawless. Nothing like a woman who rushed home from the office at five. Her makeup is perfect, red lipstick making her lips look luscious enough to bite, and her hair is in a sleep twist at the back of her neck. "Two suitcases? Is that really all?"

"How much does a person need to live for a month?"

"A month, two, who knows. I'd pack three suitcases for a week."

"That's ridiculous."

"You're right. I'm far more talented than that when it comes to clothing arrangement. I could fit three weeks' worth of outfits in one of those." Whitney steps into the entryway and gently presses the door closed behind me. I get a breath of her scent. It's light and floral, as if someone had bottled the spring air. I could breathe it for hours.

"I'm sure you could. But I don't need help packing, obviously. Where's the room?"

8

Living with Wes isn't going to be easy.

Of course, there are levels to everything. On one level, I have a handle on the rent for the next two months. A man like Wes is far too picky to decide on a place in four weeks—I can feel it in my bones.

Rent's simple. The hard part? I'm stone-cold sober, except for a half-glass of wine, and I still think he's three-mimosas hot. Hotter, even. I opened a bottle of moscato at six when he still hadn't shown up, but I'm too much of a lady to welcome a new boarder full-bottle tipsy. Especially given the three-mimosas attractiveness radiating off his cut body.

Wes clearly isn't into small talk, so I allow myself one last glance down his business-professional-clad body. The clothes do nothing to hide the muscled breadth of his shoulders, and since I've seen him shirtless semi-recently, I don't have to leave his abs to my imagination.

He looked unbelievable in a tux. He looks almost as good

wearing dress slacks and a button-up that somehow manages to bring out the color of his eyes.

"The room?" he prompts again, a hint of impatience in his eyes.

"Right. Of course. I'll give you the grand tour." The apartment I formerly shared with Summer isn't huge, but I've spent the last seventy-two hours making sure it's spotless. "In here is the living room." One couch, one overstuffed chair. Blanket thrown over the back of the couch. It looks effortless, but I spent five minutes on the arrangement. "And through here is the kitchen."

I thought about baking cookies, but he's already agreed to stay here. I'm not a fucking realtor, anyway.

"Okay." His voice is low and even. He has the kind of voice that makes me wish he'd say more, but he's apparently feeling quiet this evening.

I lead him down the hall to the bedrooms. "On the right is the bathroom. I keep towels and things in the linen closet in there, and I got a second set for you, in case you were moving in without any."

He stops outside the bathroom door and amusement brightens his green eyes. "You thought I went to *Road House*, and now you think I don't own towels?"

I lift my chin. "A courtesy, Wes Sullivan, to make your moving-in experience a little easier."

One side of his mouth quirks upward in a grin that reminds me of Summer, though I can't ever remember her being anything more than mildly sarcastic if she'd had a hard day at work. I have no idea what Wes is going to say. Something snide and asshole-ish, as is his way. "Thank you."

I wasn't expecting that, but I roll with it without even blinking. "You're welcome." I step to the end of the hall, where two doorways face each other. "I have the room on the right. This one's yours."

He looks at me, stone-faced. "I don't think so. I always take the room on the right."

What? This time, I *do* blink, lost for a witty comeback. "You might always have—" No, that's stupid. Now I've started something I can't follow through on, and there he is, staring at me while the heat rises to my cheeks. *Act, Whitney. Act.* For God's sake. This isn't any worse than the improv class I took two summers ago. "If you think—"

Wes laughs, relenting. "I'm kidding." His face relaxes and for an instant I think I'm seeing him unguarded, the way Summer must have when they were growing up together. "It's more than a little weird to be living in your sister's old room."

"What, your parents never—" Never what? Moved? Died? Caused such upheaval that you were lucky to keep your bedroom another nine months after—

"They never made us *switch*, if that's what you're asking." Wes pulls the suitcases down the hall and peers into the room. "I moved into the basement when I graduated high school. That lasted about three weeks."

We look into Summer's old room together. She left her queen-sized bed here, the mattress wrapped in an airtight protector because she lived in perpetual fear of bedbugs, but I bought a new set of sheets and a comforter to go with them. My instinct with bedding is always to get the fanciest available, but my budget prevailed. Plus, it's Wes Sullivan, not the King of England. Still, the sheets are soft enough and the comforter is a middleweight one that won't be too hot in the summer.

Not that he'll be here in the summer.

"Summer liked being on this side," I offer. "She likes the sun on her face in the morning. Hence the wide-open curtains."

Wes rolls his eyes. "The sun on her face, and yet she spent her entire childhood insisting that winter is better."

"When you're a kid, the best season is the one you're in. You haven't learned to feel the cold yet."

"Yeah."

This is veering into actual-conversation territory, and I have to say, I don't hate it.

"All right." Wes picks up the suitcases and carries them into the bedroom, setting them down with a confident *thud*. From here, he looks too big for the room, even though I know it's a fine size room for New York. God. Why do I want to push the walls outward around him, just to give him an extra few feet? It's a stupid instinct. Wes Sullivan is a man, like any other man. He doesn't get more space because he's hot and happens to have a killer body, all hard and muscled and— "Did you need something?"

"Hmm?" I've been staring at him. "Oh. No. Did *you* need something?"

He looks at me. "Some time to unpack."

That's a *Get the hell out* if I've ever heard one, but Whitney the Almost-Famous Actress takes it in stride. I smile at him, like I'm relieved to be getting away. "I'll be in the living room if you want any company."

"Good to know."

I pour myself a second glass of wine in the kitchen and settle into the couch. There's the muffled sound of dresser drawers being opened—Summer and I found them at a thrift shop and restored them one weekend, which was an entire *thing*. I'm two glasses in when he appears at the end of the hallway.

I ignore him studiously, but I can feel his eyes burning into my skin.

Wes moves into the living room.

I hold my breath and stare at the Netflix original I have playing at a low volume. Is he going to sit down next to me? Is he—

He goes past the couch to the windows.

What the hell?

Wes stands close to the frames and tests them both, then cuts back across the living room to the front door. I don't turn my head, but the sound of him yanking on the knob is unmistakable.

Okay. He wins. I stand up, wine glass in hand, and face him.

"What are you doing?"

"The security in this place is a joke. You're waiting to be robbed."

I shake my head slowly. "I choose to believe people are better than that. Not everybody who walks by my front door is a bad person."

He crosses his arms over his chest. "They're not all good, either. You can't just go through your life assuming everyone's going to be nice to you."

I scoff at him. "I would never assume that." I sit back down on the couch. "I met you, didn't I?"

Two Weeks Later

HERE'S what I can say about living with Wes Sullivan: it's a *lot* quieter than living with Summer. And she wasn't a party animal by any stretch of the imagination. I had to drag her to Vino Veritas at least every other weekend so she'd get some stimulating human contact. Not that I didn't love her homebody ways too—she had a knack for pairing wine with baked goods, and picking the best shitty movies on the planet to watch when we didn't feel like going out.

Wes doesn't do wine or shitty romcoms. He mostly does silence.

Since our little exchange over whether humanity is fundamentally decent, at the end of which I pretty much called him an asshole—*again*—he's kept a frosty distance. He leaves for work early, he comes back late, and he's quiet as a fucking mouse. I'm sure if I asked him about it, he'd say he was giving me my space.

I don't want this much space.

If I'm being honest with myself—if I'm being brutally, horribly honest with myself—the solo life isn't for me. I can put a good face on it. I can put a good face on *anything*. I have a picture of Hollywood's Man of the Year in my insurance agency cubicle, for God's sake. I am *upbeat.*

But I can't live in the silence.

Not anymore.

When I get home from work Friday night, Wes isn't there, as usual, so I slip into the shower and afterward coil my hair into a casual bun at the back of my neck. As for wardrobe, comfortable chic will do. Yoga pants, and a sweatshirt that hits very nearly at the shoulders. I look good.

I pour two glasses of moscato, then think better of it. I've got plenty of time, I know, so I head down to the bodega and buy a six-pack of beer. Not the cheapest stuff, but not break-the-bank, either.

I'm standing near the couch, poised as if I got up when I heard the door, when he gets home.

"Hey," I say, as he drops his bag on the table in the entryway and flips the lock on the door. "How was work?"

He deadbolts the door, tests it with a tug on the knob, and turns to face me. "It was fine. Some guy from my department brought bagels." He looks startled, as if he didn't plan to say this to me, but shrugs it off. An awkwardness descends between us and he clears his throat. "What about you?"

"Work was fine. I sold a lot of insurance policies." The beer is making my hand cold. "The thing is, it's too quiet in here."

He raises one eyebrow. "Too quiet?"

"I—" I always have things to say, but looking at Wes in his office outfit has me lost for words. "I didn't mean to call you an asshole the last time we talked. Not overtly."

"Last time we talked..."

"When you were telling me that this place is a prime target for robbery."

He gestures to the door. "I added a deadbolt."

"I appreciate that." I swallow. "But I only responded the way I did because it made me feel sketched out about living here, and this is my home, so I don't want to have to—"

He blows a breath out through rounded lips. "My fault. I shouldn't have made a big deal of it. I'm sure the building is perfectly safe."

"Do you want to watch a movie?" I blurt out the question because my hand is freezing, and that's the point I'm dying to get to. I want to break the ice. I want to make it comfortable to live here, and more than just in the "Rent is paid this month" kind of way. I don't expect to be best friends with Wes.

In fact, I don't want to be best friends with him.

But a conversation or two that wasn't so strained would be nice.

Wes cocks his head to the side. "You want me to watch a movie with you?"

"I got you a beer." I hold it up. "And I've furnished myself with my favorite Friday night beverage. I thought we could watch a movie together, if you didn't have any other plans."

He runs a hand through his hair. "Uh..." I must look like a hopeful puppy dog, because he relents. "Sure. Let me change out of these clothes."

"Change for as long as you want," I say, and realize a beat too late that it sounds like I'm coming on to him. Who knows? Maybe I am.

He gives me a look that's half-grin, half *what are you saying*, and retreats to the bedroom. I hear the door close and he emerges a few minutes later wearing black sweatpants and a heather gray t-shirt that looks so soft I want to bury my face in it.

"Thanks for the beer." He picks it up off the coffee table and I take a sip of wine. He cracks it open as I move to the other side of the couch. We both sit down on opposite ends.

I gather the remote. Screen on. Netflix on. "I thought we could watch this." It's a comedy from earlier in the year, something about three guys and a bachelor party that goes awry. It *should* be a decent middle ground, if Wes is the kind of person who likes to laugh once in a while. I'm not sure if he is, but I know he won't put up with a romcom, and I'm not in the mood to watch people be slaughtered for two hours.

"I heard about this," he says, voice even, and takes a sip of his beer. "Supposed to be funny."

"I'll take that as a yes."

It *is* funny. Not howl-with-laughter funny, but I laugh twice in the first thirty minutes and even hear the low rumble of Wes's chuckle at some of the shenanigans. The guys at the bachelor party end up at a resort in Mexico, nobody remembering how, and that's when the movie changes. There's a beautiful girl at the resort—isn't there always?—and all three men drool over her. The hot one gets the first chance at her, one night in the pool, her wearing an itty-bitty bikini and him wearing swim trunks that leave too much to the imagination. He says something, she says something, and then they're lip-locked in the middle of the pool.

And I'm here with Wes, watching. They're *really* going at it on the screen. I'm not embarrassed about sexuality, or a hot kiss, but heat rises to my cheeks nonetheless. Wes is silent on the other end of the couch. No. I'm not doing silence.

"Wow. He must have his tongue all the way down her throat."

"I haven't found another place yet," he answers, eyes glued to the screen.

"You are *really* good at changing the subject."

He glances over at me, honey-streaked eyes searching. Is he afraid I'll kick him out onto the street right now? "I wanted to let you know."

"So it's going to be more than a month?" That's what he's saying, but I want confirmation.

He nods crisply and turns his attention back toward the TV. "I'll stay out of your way."

"Yes. We'll both stay out of each other's way." Out of the corner of my eye, I can see him looking at me. "What?"

"You're a puzzle, Whitney."

"No, I'm not. I'm completely upfront about everything."

He laughs, a genuine sound, and the tenor of his voice sends pleasure buzzing down to the base of my spine. "Why'd you invite me to watch a movie if avoiding each other is working for you?"

Now I *must* be red. "I don't know. Maybe I only said that out of habit. I don't necessarily want to be *in* your way, either. You have a right to your own life, like I have a right to mine, but I was hoping that we wouldn't have to work *quite* so hard not to see each other, since we're living in the same apartment, and—"

"Whit."

The name on his lips sounds so familiar, so natural. "Yeah?"

"I get it." He clears his throat. "I wouldn't mind a casual conversation after work most days either."

He doesn't say anything more after that.

The texts start coming in on my phone when the movie is almost done, and I'm half-relieved to see that it's my friend Alyssa. She wants me to meet her at Vino. I don't want to turn her down.

I *want* to stay here and get to know more about Wes. I want to sit here with him and watch another movie, and then another, both of us looking forward, because I think that might be the only way he'll talk to me.

Plus, the gray t-shirt is doing a number on my lady bits. When the credits roll, I look down to discover that I've got my legs crossed tightly enough to suffocate a man. If I keep them clenched together, I definitely won't leap over to the other side of the couch and straddle Wes. *That* would be Wedding Search Two.

Not going to happen.

I get up and stretch my arms over my head, feeling his eyes on me. "That was funny."

"It was." He stands up too, wandering over to the kitchen.

"Some friends asked me to go out," I say to his back. "So I'll see you later."

"I won't wait up," he says, and laughs at his own joke.

"Smartass." It's a step down from *asshole*. His shoulders are still shaking with laughter when I go past the kitchen to my bedroom.

It takes five minutes to go from movie-night-in to wine-night-out, and when I get back to the living room, Wes is settled in on the couch, flipping through Netflix with another beer in his hand. It would be *so* easy to sit down next to him, to watch whatever he's watching.

But I don't do it.

Wes and I aren't going to be like *that*. Cordial friends, maybe. Roommates. Nothing more.

My phone buzzes with another text.

ALYSSA: **You on your way?**

WHITNEY: **Coming now!**

"Bye," I call over my shoulder as I head out the door.

"Bye," Wes says, and something in his voice makes me hesitate. Is he going to say more?

I wait five seconds, then slam the door jauntily behind me and make my way to Vino.

10

I WAS RIGHT.

Living with Whitney is excruciating.

It was bad enough trying to avoid her. Mornings were easy enough during the week. I left early, when she was still in the shower. Evenings, I stayed late.

The less I saw her, the better. The less I saw her, the less I had to see those little flashes of openness in her face. The less I had to picture those lips on mine. The less I had to work at pushing her away. She's one of those women who's so damn enthusiastic about everything, so *confident*, that you can't get them to leave you alone. Give them an inch, and they'll take a mile. Whitney can't come that close.

She can't find out what it's really like inside my head.

I thought I could handle watching a movie with her. I thought it would be easy as hell to sit there on the couch with a cold beer in hand, staring at some raunchy comedy.

I was wrong.

I could hardly follow the plot of the damn thing, if there *was* a plot, because all I could think about was her. We were only separated by a few feet. I could have reached out and touched her. I could have done more than that. If she hadn't gone out with her girlfriends...

I run a hand over my face and let out a long breath. It's time to *work*.

I can't sit here focusing on Whitney. Running all the new things I've learned about her through my mind. She works for an insurance agency, but she wants to be an actress. It partially explains her sharp wit, the way she always rolls with the punches. It doesn't explain why I find this so fucking sexy.

"Something on your mind, Sullivan?"

I spin around in my chair and face Greg, who is paused in the aisle outside my cubicle, brows knitted together with what looks like concern.

Whitney. Whitney is on my mind. Her relentless energy. The way words pour out of her, faster and faster, when she gets going. The way her mouth feels on mine. This ridiculous desire I have to know what makes her this way, to know what she's hiding.

People are always hiding something.

Greg takes my too-long pause as an invitation. "Troubles on the home front?"

I smile in spite of myself. "You mean, with my roommate?"

He waggles his eyebrows. "Yes. Your roommate. Is she giving you trouble?"

Yes. In all sorts of ways. Namely that every time I look at her, I have the strangest urge to draw her into a battle that we'll start with words and end with bodies colliding in the private space we're going to be sharing for at least the next six weeks.

"Nah. She's fine. Just making sure I've got everything lined up for this client." It's half a lie. I *was* doing that before one of the women in the office walked by wearing a pink t-shirt that reminded me of a dress Whitney has.

"You need some help?"

I hate asking for help. I hate admitting I need it. But more than that, I hate talking about Whitney. It seems gross, a violation somehow. "If you'd take a look—" I swivel back around to my computer screen and lift one of the papers from my desk. "Right here."

Greg is a helper, and he dives right in. I do my best to act like I'm paying attention.

THE AIR in the city smells like sunshine, if you can ignore the general scent of piss and garbage that runs underneath everything. I do my best to focus on the fresh air on the walk home. I try out some bullshit technique that some roving therapist gave me after the incident in the Humvee. Being aware of my surroundings, but without focusing on the negative details.

Sunshine it is.

I wish I didn't have this fucking headache.

My head throbs lightly with every step, and even though it's sunny, even though it's warm without being oppressive, I can feel my mood plummeting. Outside, by the traffic, it's too unpredictable. I want to wrap my hands around all the cars and shove them into order, silence the cab drivers shouting at each other.

On the last corner before the apartment, some asshole runs a red light and almost gets nailed, the brakes screeching. They're shitty brakes and the metal-on-metal scream makes my heart beat faster, adrenaline running its fingers up the length of my spine.

The pressure in my temples intensifies.

What the fuck is wrong with me? A car braking, narrowly missing another car, and a man shouting at the top of his lungs, his speech laced with a foreign accent, and I'm breaking out into a sweat that's hardly appropriate for a gentle spring day in Manhattan.

I clench my fist around the handle of my bag and watch the walk signal across the street. Living here, like this, was supposed to make this better.

It's getting worse every day.

I'VE ALMOST GOT it under control by the time I step into the apartment. All the lights are off and it's blessedly dark. With the locks shut behind me, the pounding pressure in my chest eases a little bit.

I put my bag on the table and take a breath.

Whitney is silhouetted against the big window behind the television, mouthing words that I assume are written on the paper she's clutching with both hands. She must have another audition. When she's not running out for wine with her friends, or inviting me to casual movie nights where we sit on the couch and try not to stray into uncomfortable territory, she's practicing for auditions.

She makes a hideous face, teeth bared, mouth stretched open.

I can't help myself. "You'll never get the part with that face."

Whitney glances over, her face neutral, not at all surprised to see me. "It was good enough for you to kiss," she says dismissively, then goes right back into the hideous expression. "So I'd shut my mouth, if I were you."

"Maybe you should shut it for me." Oh, my God. It's like the headache has dissolved the filter that normally keep idiocy like this from coming out of my mouth.

Whitney looks across at me, eyebrows raised. "Yes, because that worked out so well for me before."

"Didn't it? I went to the wedding."

She scrunches up her face into a smile. "And thank goodness, because you were a joy and a delight to all involved."

"Please. You liked it."

"Are you talking about the part at the reception where you were an ass to me?" Whitney's tone is still light, but there's a seriousness to her words that takes me aback. "I wouldn't say that I *liked* it. I liked that you decided to be there for Summer." She looks back down at the paper. I'd bet anything she's pretending to read it. "As for the rest..." Whitney shrugs.

"Are you serious?" I laugh out loud, bewildered, and suddenly I don't care about boundaries. I don't care about pushing her away. No, I want to draw her in closer. I want to know what's really going on in that head of hers. Hot and cold. Sarcastic and vulnerable. Which one is the real Whitney? "I saw how you looked at me the day I moved in."

"You were mistaken," she says primly. "I was hot for that rent money." Whitney moves into the living room, her face shadowed. She's like a magnet. I step out of the entryway, stand at the edge of the couch.

"You're a liar."

"You wouldn't know."

Whitney's facing off with me, arms crossed, paper crumpled in her hand. A slow smile spreads across her face. "What is this, Wes? What kind of day has it been?"

"What kind of *day*?"

"Yeah." She shifts her weight from one foot to the other, and the movement of her hips is so distracting it's hard to haul my eyes away from the curve of her waist and back up to her eyes. "What kind of day would make you come home like this? Such aggressive jokes."

Whitney grins at me, and I have no idea what the hell is going on, but I know what I want it to be.

"Such aggressive lying," I counter. "I saw how you looked at me that first day I moved here, and I saw how you looked at me when we were watching that stupid movie."

"That movie was funny."

She steps toward me and I take a breath. The air in here is light and clean, like she's opened a window, and on top of it is the scent of her, fresh and bright and utterly intoxicating.

"If you know I'm lying, then prove it." Whitney lifts her chin. I could reach out and take it in my hand right now. "One kiss. Right now."

We're *way* over the line. *Way.*

"I don't fuck around with roommates."

She takes another step closer. "I'm not fucking around."

We are inches apart.

"That's not true, and you know it."

Whitney cocks her head to the side, her dark eyes endless in the cool light of the living room. "I don't have anything to prove." She raises one shoulder an inch, then lowers it.

Every inch of me wants to close that infuriating distance between us and take her, right here on the floor. There's nothing stopping us. She's not about to walk down the aisle in professional makeup and a bridesmaid's dress that has to be spotless. The door is locked. The only thing I'd be crossing is the line we drew in the sand.

"Good," I tell her. "I'm late to meet someone anyway."

11

ABSOLUTELY NONE of my attention should be on Wes Sullivan.

Almost all of it is.

It's stupid. It's really fucking stupid, because I have a life to lead. A wonderful, glorious life, full of auditions that will almost certainly lead to me getting rejected and sales calls that, thirty percent of the time, result in no benefit for either party involved.

I have no *idea* what happened yesterday. It was Thursday. We've lived together for two Thursdays, and at first, when he turned his back on me and walked out, I thought he was lying about meeting with someone.

Once my heart stopped pounding, I smoothed out the audition script and forced myself to think clearly. He left last Tuesday after work too, for about an hour and a half. Never said where he was going. He doesn't *have* to say where he's going, obviously, but clearly, he has some kind of standing obligation.

I turn it over in my mind while I walk down to Vino, the noontime sun warm on my shoulders. It's warm enough to get away with a light jacket or a sweater. I love the sun.

But I hate this time of year. The way the light angles down onto the sidewalks, sweet and fresh, makes my heart ache. It weighs heavy inside my chest.

As much as I don't want to spend time praising Eva Lipton for her success as a writer when I, Whitney Coalport, haven't so much as landed a callback this month, it'll be a good distraction.

Hopefully.

I stop outside Vino and put a smile on that doesn't match how heavy and down I feel, then pull open the door and rush inside. Fake it 'til you make it. That's acting. That's life.

When Eva and I were in high school together, she was as dramatic as I was, only about books. She was obsessed with books. She couldn't get *enough* of them. She made friends with the school librarian the instant she stepped foot in the high school. Eva had an enormous mane of curly red hair, braces, and freckles for days.

I almost don't recognize her when she stands up from the table she's snagged at Vino, beaming at me.

"Oh, my *God*," she says, her voice a lower, more mature version of the chipmunk-like chatter she used to spout all day long about what she was reading. I didn't mind it back then because I talked just as much about what we were doing in theater. Theater made my soul sing. Thankfully, most of the tapes I had from our old shows are long gone, because the *actual* singing could reasonably be described as atrocious. "Whitney! I can't believe it. You're so glamorous."

Eva holds her arms out for a hug, and as I go in for it, I look her up and down as surreptitiously as possible. She's taller than I remembered, about my height, and all the baby fat that clung to her face as a teenager is gone. She's tamed her frizzy red curls into a magnificent auburn waterfall spilling over her shoulders, the pieces at her face held back with an elegant clip. We hug, and it's warm and natural, and then I push her back so I can look at her again.

"Me? Are you kidding?" I'm not going to mention that I spent twenty minutes on my makeup before this lunch date. Anything to compete with her unbelievable success. "You're the glamor girl! Your hair is so—"

She fluffs it with her hands. "Not shitty anymore?" Then she laughs, and it takes me all the way back to high school, to our corner in the library, to her stack of books next to my stack of scripts. Her laugh is still exactly the same. "I know. It took years, but I finally figured out how *not* to look like a complete crazy moron."

That makes me laugh. "You never looked like a crazy moron."

"You're awfully kind, Whit, but I've seen pictures." *Whoa,* she mouths, eyes huge, and laughs again. "Is this table okay?"

"This table's perfect." What's even more perfect is the open bottle of white already there. We slide into seats across from one another and Eva lets out a huge breath. I pour myself a glass and settle in, the sparkling sweetness dancing on my tongue. "You look a little overwhelmed," I tell her with a grin.

"Oh, I am. I *am*. New York City is *nothing* like the old Grove."

It's what we used to call Buffalo Grove, the suburb of Chicago we grew up in, and at the mention of the town, my chest constricts. I smile bigger to cover it up. "No. They're not kidding when they say the city never sleeps."

Eva groans. "Never. There's always *something* going on, and the light pollution is unbelievable."

I giggle at that. "It can't be that much worse than at home."

"It *is*. Well—" She looks sheepish. "At home, my bedroom overlooked our backyard pool. My parents kept it pitch dark out there for optimal sleeping conditions."

"My bedroom was up front," I say. "I liked the way the street-light came through the curtain."

She nods and sips at her wine. "You must be used to it, then."

"The light? Yeah. Other things, not so much."

Eva's eyes light up and she leans in. "That sounds cryptic. Tell me everything immediately."

"Oh, there's nothing to tell. Just roommate drama."

"Now you *have* to tell me. I love drama. Writing about it, anyway."

A lowkey excitement threads its way through my veins. It's like my entire brain is glowing from the opportunity to talk to an old friend. We've slipped back into those patterns, like college never happened, like moving to opposite sides of the country never happened. With a pang, I realize how much I've been missing Summer since she moved in with Dayton...and how I can't get this kind of connection from Wes.

"It's kind of a long story."

"I don't have any other plans," Eva coaxes. "Tell me!"

I take a deep breath.

"It started with my roommate, Summer."

"Very intriguing." She leans back in her seat and listens intently while I tell her about meeting Summer in college, about reconnecting with her when she needed a place to live in the city, about the crazy love she and Day share. I do my best not to sound jealous. Eva nods in all the right places.

"Anyway, after she moved out, it's been one weirdo after another in the apartment. I don't have enough money to cover the rent by myself, so I had to find a roommate. The current one is..." I let my voice trail off. I don't know if I want to get into this.

"Who?" Eva sounds breathless.

"It's Summer's older brother."

"Oooooh," she says, expression going hopeful. "Is he hot?"

"No," I say instinctively, but then I give in. "Yes. He's ridiculously hot."

Eva puts her wine glass down on the table and looks me dead in the eye. "Whitney. First, show me a picture right now. Second, tell me you're taking advantage of this sexy man meat living under your roof."

The wine is already spreading warmth everywhere it touches, and I crack up. "Sexy *man meat*." I laugh so hard I shed a tear over it. "I can't believe you said that."

"Photo evidence," she demands.

"I don't think I—" I take out my purse. "Wait. I do. You're so lucky we were in a wedding together."

"Your friend's wedding?"

I scroll through the pictures Summer sent me, including one of me and Wes on the dance floor. It's mostly of him, looking down at me, his face caught between a smirk and a laugh, and he looks fucking delicious. Even though he was being a total dick at the time. Eva holds her hand out for the phone and I give it.

"Sweet lord," she says softly, giving it a good long look before she hands it back. "Jump on that. You have to." She nods to back up her point. "*Have* to."

I roll my eyes up toward the ceiling. "Been there, done that."

"Oh, my *God*." Eva slaps her hands down on the surface of the table. "You *did*?"

"I went after him at Summer's wedding. Mimosas," I say, as if this explains everything, and Eva accepts it as a legitimate excuse for why I kissed Wes in an effort to get him to attend. "It didn't end *super* well."

"Why? Is he a prick?"

"I'd say so," I tell her, but a small part of me feels like this is a betrayal. Wes can be cold, but I have a nagging suspicion that there's more to him than that. I know there is. I've seen flashes of it.

"Still," says Eva.

"Still," I tell her.

We sip our wine in silent agreement.

~

I'M on the drunk side of tipsy when I get back to the apartment.

Wes is cooking.

I'm hit with a spicy, fragrant stir-fry scent as soon as I walk in the door. It makes my stomach growl even though we ordered three appetizers between us, damn it. I kick off my shoes and saunter into the kitchen, bracing my hands against the doorframe.

Wes is standing at the stove, his back to me, hands moving easily over a chopping board. He doesn't turn, doesn't look. Maybe he didn't hear me come in. He finishes dicing what-ever he's chopping up and tips it into the crackling pan on the stove. Jesus, it smells good.

"Why the hell were you trying to get me to kiss you again?"

The question isn't nearly as eloquent as I would have liked, but at the sound of my voice, Wes whips his head around, eyebrows raised. One corner of his mouth lifts in a little smirk. "I see you had a good time."

I stand up tall, hands on my hips. "Answer the question."

He shrugs carelessly, and I don't expect an honest answer. "You were there the first time. It was hot."

My expectations are *always* off, aren't they? "That wasn't hot. That was desperate." My tongue feels like a lead weight in my mouth. Maybe I'm a little more than tipsy.

"Does that matter?" He turns sideways, stirring at the pan with one hand so he can look at me.

"Yes."

"Why?" His question sounds genuine enough.

"That was a special case. I was saving the day for Summer. It didn't mean anything."

"A kiss doesn't need meaning to be sexy as hell."

"If it was so sexy, why were you such an ass?"

The smirk disappears, and with a *thud* to my gut, I realize he's being honest. Only I don't know if I want him to be honest. I don't know if I want to see the real Wes now, today. "I couldn't let you get any closer."

It hurts to hear him say that. It shouldn't, but it does, a sting that ricochets across my ribs and dives down into my stomach. "I only wanted you to get close enough to come to the wedding." I fling the words at him dismissively.

He clicks his tongue and turns back to the stove. "So harsh."

"It's the truth. And I'm not hungry."

I *am* hungry. I'm starving. I want him to offer me a plate of whatever he's cooking more than anything in the world in this moment, but I'm stewing in hurt and delayed-onset jealousy and the kind of angst I thought I'd left behind in my high-school locker. Fuck. I hate this.

"Good," Wes says mildly, with one glance over his shoulder. "Because none of this is for you."

I leave without another word, dragging one hand along the wall to keep myself upright. I brush my teeth in the bathroom and retreat to my bedroom, where I lay down, fully clothed.

None of this is for you.

It never is, is it?

12

I stop dead in the hallway outside the bathroom.

Sunday afternoon, golden sunlight streams in every available window of the apartment, illuminating a scene I never *once* thought I'd see. It's like something out of the world's tamest porno, if your porn of choice was a lingerie magazine.

I've been out all day. I went for a run in Central Park. I ate lunch in a diner. I generally avoided Whitney, because holy *shit* was last night awkward. Her wine date must've put her up to something, because she came in with her verbal fists swinging, putting a name to the tension that's been thick in our apartment since she told me to my face that she doesn't have the hots for me.

Fat fucking chance.

I was honest with her last night when I shouldn't have been. I've been giving her space.

She's been doing laundry.

I must've known deep down that this would happen eventually. We're living with each other for the convenience of it, and since I've moved in, we've always done laundry on different days. Usually, she's folding it in a basket when I get back from my weekly appointments at the VA. Half the time, I actually go. Half the time, I go to the park and walk around the big loop.

None of that matters.

Whitney isn't here, but the bathroom is *full* of her bras.

The girl has a magnificent fucking collection.

It's an expensive rainbow of lingerie, ranging from black to aqua to red, and they're all hanging up around the bathroom, taunting me.

I'm rooted to the spot, pinned in place by thoughts I can't stop.

Was she wearing one of these at the wedding? Was the lacy fabric grazing her nipples, making them hard, when she leapt at me, pressing her mouth against mine? Are these what Whitney wears under her shirt every *day*, while she's wearing her demure dresses that flare at the hips, or the button-downs and dress slacks that make her ass look so grabbable I have to keep my hands in my pockets?

I'm harder than iron at the thought, my cock pressing painfully against the zipper of my work pants. This is some fucking fantasy, and for once, I don't mind letting my imagination run away with me. For once, it's running toward something soft and sexy, not toward the killing fields of Afghanistan. For once.

My eyes settle on a deep purple bra, a jewel hanging over

the curtain rod. I've never been much for purple, but I can practically see it against her creamy skin. The only thing sexier than seeing her delectably round, full breasts rising above the line of this bra would be taking it off. Undoing the hooks, one by one. Slipping my fingers underneath the straps, drawing them over her shoulders one after the other, until this purple thing made of lace and lust falls to the floor and those fucking gorgeous breasts spill out into my hands.

She'd gasp at my touch, the pads of my thumbs against her nipples, and that's all it would take. One arch of her back and all the sunshine and sarcasm would fall away. She'd be the woman who kissed me in my hotel room. She'd be dark and hot and mine.

I take in a ragged breath.

"What are you doing?"

Oh, fuck.

Whitney stands in the hallway in a t-shirt and yoga pants, laundry basket balanced against her hip, a little smile on her face that looks so smug I want to kiss it off. "You know, they're a lot sexier when they're on."

"I'm on my way to my room." My voice is gruff. I'm fucking caught with a tent in my pants I have zero hope of hiding.

She nods sagely. "Yes. Better take care of yourself." I watch her gaze flick down to the front of my pants.

This should be one-hundred percent humiliating, but even in this moment, even in this embarrassing fucking moment, I want more than her eyes on the outline of my cock pushing against my pants. I want her on her knees, that hopeful smile playing on her lips. That's what I want. This is as close as it's going to get. So it's only ninety percent humiliating.

Fuck.

Whitney turns her head, averting her eyes, and I take the moment to escape down the hallway and into my bedroom. I shut the door as quietly as I can. She doesn't need to know the animalistic need raging through my veins.

She caught me.

She fucking caught me, and there was no way to avoid it. I might as well have been standing there with my pants down. I wish it had ended in both of us on the floor, her basket spilled onto the carpet.

But I'm in here, wanting to fuck her so badly I can taste it, and she's probably in the bathroom, putting up more bras to taunt me when I walk back out.

If I walk back out.

I run both hands over my face, willing this to go away.

It doesn't.

I can't get any of it out of my head. The lingerie. The curve of her hip jutting against that laundry basket. The red lips in a little smile, dark eyes locked on me.

I grip the edge of the dresser with one hand and unzip with the other. There's no way I can live with this. My fucking head's going to explode. I'm so on edge that it can't take more than a minute of hard strokes before I'm grabbing for a tissue like a teenager. Part of me cares. The rest of me shudders with the release.

My heart slows, and I sit down heavily on my bed. I can still taste how much I want her, but at least the pressure in my head—and everywhere else—has loosened its grip.

There's a casual knock on my bedroom door. "Wes?"

"I'm good." Jesus Christ.

"Did you want any Chinese? I'm going to order from the place down the street."

"I'm good." I lie back on the bed and close my eyes. "I'm fine."

"You sure?"

The last of my resolve snaps like an old rubber band. "Go away, Whitney."

She does.

13

"SORRY TO BE CALLING with less-than-ideal news, but we'll get the next one. I just know it!"

I take a breath in and let it out silently, so Christy doesn't hear. "You know what they say about the cookie crumbling." I tack a mild chuckle onto the end, so she knows I'm still in this game, still rolling with the punches.

But this feels like a knife to the gut, deflating the last possible balloon of positivity I had going into today.

May first.

I tried to hold it off, I really did. I went to an impromptu improv class last night and absolutely killed it. The rest of the group was in stitches at the end of my last sketch. Their laughter rolled over me and buoyed my spirits.

For all of an hour.

This morning, I woke up with an ache in my throat like the beginning of sickness, only it's not that. It's not allergies, either. I've been taking my allergy pills religiously since we had the first melt at the end of February.

This day, every year, is the biggest acting job of my life.

Honestly, I was doing pretty well until Christy called with more bad news. Any other day, I could have brushed it off as a fact of the business, but today? Today, it pins me to my chair, weighing my hips down with defeat. Lucky for me, Helen's birthday lunch has already come and gone. I was the life of the party then too. If the call had come any earlier, it would have been a disaster.

I try to smile at Hollywood's Man of the Year. Tears come to my eyes instead.

I suffer through the final hour of cold calls, feeling a tiny flash of triumph when I sell an insurance policy to a prickly woman who spends fifteen minutes grilling me about different scenarios involving a rental home she and her husband were thinking of selling. But that, too, was like a balloon filled with lead instead of air.

I fucking hate this day.

It sucks the light out of everything around it.

By the time I stand up from my desk to make the beautiful, sunshine-soaked walk home, I can feel my shoulders slouching. I press them upward, against this complicated grief, and grin through it all the way out the front doors.

It's delicious, early May in New York City. We're not at the point yet where it's all overheated garbage and broken air conditioners, and I breathe in what little sweetness I can find on the walk back home.

It's not enough.

I need a pick-me-up.

I stop at the grocery store two blocks from home, covering this ridiculous grief, this ludicrous sadness, with an animal need for sweet & salty Chex Mix and a package of Rolos. I want to dump the Chex Mix into a bowl and eat all the cookie sticks and cookie whorls first, leaving the pretzels for whatever poor sucker gets to the bag after me. I want to unwrap the Rolos one by one, tearing the golden foil into a neat curlicue, and fill the gaping void in my gut with chocolate and caramel.

I take a basket from the stand at the front and move through the aisles. Don't look at anyone. Don't make eye contact. It's not my usual game, but I feel like I'm teetering on the edge of something vast and unpleasant. Chex Mix, check. Rolos, check. But I shouldn't leave here with a bunch of junk food. The sight of these things alone in my cart takes me to another level of sorrow and guilt, and I swallow a hard lump in my throat, tears stinging at the corners of my eyes.

Jesus Christ.

I blink them away. Add some bananas, and it'll be okay. Maybe a single red apple.

I'm standing in front of the produce section, searching for yellow in a sea of green bananas, when an old woman pushes her cart up next to me. "I'm looking for pineapple," she says tremulously. "The kind in the can, but I can't find it. I've been looking everywhere."

It's an innocent question but her voice barrels through the last of what was holding me together.

I press my lips tight, trying to summon the instructions for the pineapple. *They're in Aisle 3.* I open my mouth, but what comes out is, "I'm sorry."

That's all.

I put the basket down on the floor at my feet and leave empty-handed. I walk fast, all the way back to the apartment, trying to outrun it.

Wes is cooking again.

Fuck that guy.

I slam the door behind me and the first sob escapes; a guttural, ugly cry.

He comes to the door of the kitchen as I'm running past to the bedroom.

"Are you okay?"

"Don't fucking worry about it," I spit at him.

"Whitney—"

In my bedroom, I throw myself across the bed like I'm fifteen years old and cry into the pillow, so hard that it makes my head hurt, so hard that when it's over, I don't even turn my head. I just fall asleep.

A SOFT KNOCK on the door wakes me.

What time is it? The bedroom is dusky, the light fading outside the window.

"Whit?" The way Wes says my name reminds me of

Summer. How could it not? They grew up together. They have a lot of similar habits, even if they don't realize it. The ache in my chest expands again and I breathe it out while I sit up in bed. "Are you awake?"

"Yeah." I sound hoarse as balls, and I'm tangled up in my pencil skirt. I'm still trying to figure out how exactly to get it to release my legs when the door opens. Wes stands halfway inside, framed by the soft light from the hallway. "What time is it?"

"It's almost eight." He sticks his hands in his pockets. "I've got some extra chicken, if you're hungry."

I want to deny it, but my stomach growls. "I'm having a shitty day." Damn it. My voice wavered on *day* and now I'm about to lose it again. Buck up, buttercup. "So if you're here to fuck with me—"

"I'm not here to fuck with you. I have dinner, if you're interested. Thought you might want to—"

"Want to what?" I feel defensive, crouched back like a cat, even though I'm just sitting here on top of the covers, in a pencil skirt that's seen better days. "Find somewhere else to eat?"

Wes laughs, the sound adjacent to kindness. "No. I thought you might want to step into the shower and put on some comfortable clothes. It can't be comfortable sleeping in those office clothes. Plus, your hair—" He motions around his head.

I raise a hand to my hair. It's tangled, somehow, half fallen out of the bun I was wearing it in. "Oh. Right."

"I'll get you a towel." He disappears back into the hallway

and reappears a moment later, a clean towel hanging from his hand. I smile at that. He had to go into the bathroom for it, where I will be going in a matter of moments. Still, it's almost sweet. "Food's on the table whenever you're ready."

I toss myself awkwardly out of bed and take the towel. "Why are you doing this?" I'm still half-drunk from sleep and I can't stop myself from asking the question.

Wes cocks his head to the side. "You came home in tears. Something's up. I don't know what it is, but you could use some food, at least."

I am wretched, mean, and small, and embarrassment coats my cheeks with pink. "Why do you care?"

"Because you're my roommate," says Wes, but his eyes say something different. "I'm not *that* much of a dick."

When Wes said *chicken,* I assumed he meant exactly what he said.

It's not that.

I sit down at a place at the kitchen table and look it over. It's chicken drenched in what looks like—

"Is this a red wine sauce?"

Wes puts a plate of dinner rolls in the center of the table and sits down. "Yeah."

"I thought you meant plain chicken."

He raises one eyebrow. "Who eats plain chicken?"

"Men, I thought."

Wes takes some food for himself, filling his plate, and I stare at it. There is a vegetable. There are rolls. This is an entire *meal.*

"Come on," he says. "It'll get cold."

It's good food. Really good food, buttery and sauce-y, and nothing like what I expected. We eat in silence, sitting across from one another, but it doesn't feel strained. It feels almost normal.

Until Wes puts his fork down and sighs, as if he's been holding something in this entire time. "Look. I never say this kind of thing, but if you want to talk about it—"

A bite of chicken sticks in my throat. I do *not* want to talk about it, ever, but there's something about the way he's looking at me that makes me want to get it out in the open. I'm too tired to lie anyway. "My dad died when I was eighteen."

"Oh, *shit,*" Wes says softly.

"Yeah." I stab a butter-soaked carrot with my fork. "We'd been fighting a lot. He was kind of a dick in a lot of ways." He was. He was volatile and moody, and when his mood was low, things were hard. But when it was high, it was the best ever. "He didn't think I should go away to college, and we fought about it. I told him to fuck off." He'd laughed at me. My dad had laughed, a sound of surprise and delight, and it had pissed me off at the time. "He was working a weird shift at that time, and got hit by a drunk driver on his way home."

Wes puts a hand to his forehead. "That's fucking rough."

It can't be nearly as rough as going to war. I know about the incident with the Humvee, but only the vague details... something Summer said in passing once.

"It still gets to me every year. I try—" I swallow hard. "I try, you know, to remember that life is short, and that it blows to spend it being angry and sad, but some days it's hard."

"Is there anything that makes you feel better?"

Who *is* this version of Wes? This version of Wes who cares what the hell I think, how I feel?

"I tried to get sweet & salty Chex mix and candy at the store, but I failed. Some old lady pushed me over the edge."

"Old ladies will do that. Anything else?" His eyes are on mine, gentle, not a hint of the animosity that sometimes flashes there.

"Watching you eye-grope my bras made me feel better." My mouth pulls upward in a smile. That was *hilarious*.

Wes rolls his eyes. "You're never going to let me forget that."

"I will if you agree to watch a shitty movie with me."

"Right now?"

"Right now."

We take our plates to the couch and Wes lets me pick some obnoxious romcom that lightens my soul. Halfway through, the plates pushed away onto the coffee table, he slips his arm around me. God, it feels good, a comforting weight. There's no pressure there.

"Is this the part where we kiss again?" The couple on the screen is playing in the water on some Mexican beach, the woman in a bikini that looks like it could fall off at any moment.

Wes leans in and silvery anticipation sweeps through my veins, but he only kisses me on the temple. "I don't fuck around with girls who are going through a bad day."

"Oh, but you'll put your arm around me? Wow, that's—"

He tugs at his arm, but I lock my hand around his wrist and pull it back, leaning into the solid warmth of him.

We stay that way for the rest of the movie, not saying a word.

14

WES

I'VE NEVER SEEN her like that before.

I wake up the next morning still thinking about it—the sorrow in Whitney's face. A drunk driver? Fuck. That's the kind of thing nobody can prepare for. I pulled plenty of dumb stuff as a teenager, fought with my parents plenty of times, but it makes my chest feel strange to think about ending things with them on that kind of note.

I want to kiss the pain away.

Whitney can be infuriating. That energy of hers, bright and unceasing, gives me a headache if it hits the wrong way. I saw it for what it was last night—an act. I'm sure there's a layer to it that's real. I'm sure, deep down, she's a sunny-as-hell person. I didn't count on the darkness at the heart of it.

The sound of the shower permeates my thoughts and I squint at the bedside table. It's too early. She must be slipping away before I get up. It was intense, last night, sitting that close, gathering her into my side and not doing anything else.

That's all it takes to take my morning wood from half-hearted to raging. I could have laid her back on the couch, I could have stripped off those yoga pants, I could have breathed in the scent of her, my face inches from her panties...

I wait until the apartment door clicks shut to get out of bed.

I'm not going into work this morning. I have a bullshit appointment at the VA and lunch with Dayton, but something Whitney said last night is still nagging at me. She tried to pull herself out of it—she stopped at the store, but didn't make it to the checkout.

That fucking *blows.* And I'm going to make it right.

I shower and dress, then walk down to the bodega in the silky morning air. The owner—I can never remember his name—nods at me. What was she talking about? Chex Mix.

There are about a hundred varieties of Chex Mix, but the one she wanted isn't there. Oh—wait. No, it's here, wedged all the way in the bottom corner of the shelf. Sweet & Salty.

Next on my list: candy.

She didn't say what kind, and I linger in the aisle for long enough to get frustrated. Skittles? Sure. A Milky Way? Why not? I grab four candy bars at random. At the end of the aisle, a package of Rolos catches my eye. I swear I've seen her eating these. I add it to the stack of things in my hands.

The apartment is still silent when I open the door, and I'm half-disappointed. It's good that she felt up to going to work, but I wouldn't have minded another chance to be near her. I want to be here to see her face when she sees these things and laugh out loud. What am I going to do, hang around here all day waiting, in case she comes home early?

No. There's a gravitational pull to stay here, to be close in case she needs me, but even the Earth doesn't crash into the sun for the love of it.

There's a cereal dish in the sink that nags at me. I spend fifteen minutes in the kitchen, moving out toward the living room.

Everything is tidy. I'm out of excuses.

I go to the meeting.

~

"I don't have a problem."

Dr. O'Connors, who can't be more than nineteen, raises his eyebrows. "The things you're describing indicate to me that daily life has become a struggle."

I let out an irritated breath. "Daily life is fine since I moved to the city."

Except the traffic. Always the traffic. All the prick drivers in the city seem to follow me around every day, running into each other, fender-benders that are so easily avoidable. If they'd look, for five seconds—

Like a condescending asshole, he flips through his notes. "You've mentioned difficulty riding the train."

"I walk to work now." Not that it ever gets me away from the fucking traffic. The cars might as well be in this exam room with us, since this guy won't let the topic drop.

"Yes. You've become adept at avoiding the kinds of situations that you think might trigger you, but my concern is that the symptoms might find another outlet."

I open my mouth and shut it again. Now is not the time to mention the way my head pounds when I get home from work most days. It's also not the time to mention the way I have to wear headphones on the walk, because the sound of traffic sets me off. It's the yelling. It's exactly like that sound after the Humvee hit that IED, when everything was chaos. The longer I listen, the more it blurs into my fellow soldiers. I'm not going to fucking say a word, because then he'll say that I have—

"My feeling is that you're dealing with post-traumatic stress disorder. I see you were involved with an incident during one of your deployments that would cause anyone to—"

I groan out loud. "I don't have PTSD. These are only thoughts. I was deployed four times."

He looks at me over his clipboard, levelly, and then continues on as if I haven't said a thing. "I'm recommending a course of anti-anxiety medications and talk therapy. We can begin with something low-dose and see if—"

"No." No way. Not a fucking chance. I'm not taking pills. I don't have PTSD. I have memories, like every other human being on the planet. "I'm not taking pills. You can stop writing that down right now, because I'm never going to do it."

"Fine." He keeps writing. "I'm referring you to a very well-regarded psychologist in the building. In fact"—O'Connors swivels on his little black stool to the computer in the corner of the room—"she has an opening for next Wednesday. It is now yours. The appointment will last about an hour."

"Great." I stand up. "Is there anything else?" My heart rockets against my rib cage. I'm not going to this fucking appointment. I'm not going to talk about what happened in the Humvee. If they want to know what happened, they can look up my official records. That's the end of that. I'm not going back there. I'm not.

O'Connors blinks up at me. "Do you have any other concerns?"

"Not a single thing," I tell him, and then I turn my back and leave.

"THAT LITTLE PRICK at the VA is too much," I tell Dayton over burgers. He picked this place. It looked fancier than it is, but the food is good, so I haven't given him too much shit about his high-class ways.

"Did you have a thing today?"

"Yeah." I sigh and take another bite of my burger. "It was bullshit. As usual. But what the hell else am I supposed to do?" Day knows what I'm talking about. The appointments at the VA take forever to set up. Miss one and you're back in a quagmire of red tape. I have no idea how he skirted all of it, because I know he wasn't showing up regularly when he got his leg fixed.

"Dr. Peterson?"

"O'Connors. God. That guy has a head bigger than the continental U.S."

Dayton laughs. "He's not so bad. Got on my nerves too, until I got over myself."

Dayton—he's the one who came out of this with a real injury. He's the one who lost his left leg below the knee. I'm not going to go cry to some shrink over the fact that I made it through four deployments with scratches and bruises that have long since faded.

"I don't want anything to do with it." I swirl a fry around in a puddle of ketchup. "Screw it."

I can feel Dayton looking at me across the table. He's been my best friend since we were kids, so I know he's giving me that stare, trying to figure out what's going on in my head. I eat another fry and refuse to look at him. By the time I glance up, his attention is back on his burger. "It's not that bad," he says lightly.

"What's not?"

"The talk therapy bull," he says. "It's really cut down on some of the things that were bothering me."

He waves vaguely around his head. I don't have to ask what he means. I know about the nightmares. Fuck, everyone does. There's not a single man I know who's come back from combat without dreams that make the sheets seem like they're trying to suffocate you. It's the cost of doing business.

I take a bite of burger, chew it, swallow. They're *good* here, thick and juicy and solid, and after all that bullshit at the appointment, it's what I need to ground me.

"That's good," I admit. "But you're the only one who came back with a problem."

Day eyes me across the table, hands wrapped around the remaining half of his burger. "Not likely."

I look right back at him. "I still have both my legs."

"You were in the Humvee, same as I was." There's more than one meaning here, but he's being as stubborn as O'Connors. I don't have a problem. Everybody I know wants to tell me I have a problem, but I don't. I went to Summer's wedding, for God's sake. I got a job in the city. I'm doing everything they wanted me to do. Who the fuck cares if I walk to work, the music turned up loud?

I roll my eyes, an exaggerated move calculated to make Dayton laugh, and it works. "You're not going to convince me I'm crazy."

He grins back at me. "I don't have to convince you or anybody else of that. I *know* you're crazy. I've known you since we did Midnight at Suicide Mountain."

I laugh out loud. "That was more a risk than the Humvee."

I'd forgotten about Midnight at Suicide Mountain, an ill-advised film Day and I shot on an old-ass camera we found in his dad's basement. We went to Suicide Hill behind the school in the middle of the night one winter, lit some cheap sparklers left over from the Fourth of July, and went down on saucers, blind into the night. Could have broken our necks.

"See? Who needs more proof than that? You should let O'Connors know you've always been that stupid."

"Sure. If I see him again, which I won't, knowing how the VA works. They'll call me up sometime next year, wondering where I went."

"I like the leg they got for me," says Day, digging into his fries.

"They only gave back what they took in the first place," I say in a mock-serious voice.

He opens his mouth to say something but outside the window, twenty feet away, a guy runs out into the street in front of a yellow cab. I see a flash of his red coat, turn my head, and there's that metal-on-metal screech. The impact comes a second later—a delivery truck, beat up as hell, running into the cab. Neither of them is going fast but I hear it, the crunch, as it reverberates through the restaurant window. The Humvee lifts up under my hands, the heat blooming through the underside, and there's a second of silence before Dayton screams, an ugly, strangled thing. I'm drenched in sweat. It's a spring day but there's desert heat whipping in past the glass, gritty and stinking with fear and sweat.

"—for a beer? Wes? Wes."

I turn my head away from the scene in front of my eyes and back toward Dayton. He looks at me with narrowed eyes, one hand on the surface of the table, mid-reach. A surge of anger rises, covering the fear, blocking it out. "Yeah? Jesus. What? I heard you."

An infinitesimal shake of his head. He doesn't believe me. "I said, do you want to go for a beer or do you have to get back?"

The anger dissolves. There's no fucking way I can sit at my desk like this. "Let's go for a beer." I get up, everything stiff and weird. "I'll go back once we've had a beer."

15

THE ARRANGEMENT on the coffee table could only be from the version of Wes I met last night. The one with kindness at the core of him. Last night, I met the version of Wes who was raised in the same household as Summer, who learned how to care for people in an atmosphere of love instead of loss, and who carried that with him, even during his stint in the Army.

I almost pass out from the sheer patriotism swelling in my chest, the pure swooning love for timeless American values, for this small-town *thing* he has going on, before I pull myself out of it.

Or at least I try to.

I don't go for this kind of guy. I like the moody blues, the powerful executives who moonlight in shitty bars, men with a complicated view of the world. I thought Wes was simple, selfish.

Yet there's a bag of Chex Mix on the table, Sweet & Salty, the kind I like. Five different candies, including the Rolos I was pining after, are fanned out around it. And a *Vitamin Water*. He didn't forget the drink.

This isn't the mark of a selfish man.

Beyond that, the apartment is spotless. I can still smell the lemon scent of the cleaning solution we keep under the counter. Has he been here recently? Did he do this before he left for work? I get the whole neat-as-a-pin attitude, no doubt coming from his days in the Army, but this is beyond.

I wander into the living room, looking for something to straighten, but not so much as a pillow is out of place.

There are flowers too.

It's a little bouquet from the bodega, the kind they keep by the cold drinks for a few dollars, but it's bright and happy, stuck into a little vase he must've found under the sink. It's not the kind of bouquet you'd get for someone on, say, Valentine's Day. It doesn't scream *I'm trying to impress you*. It screams something else entirely. A friendship bouquet?

Heat rises to my cheeks. Sure. I've never had a friendship this tense.

I pick up the bag of Chex Mix and hold it in my hands. It shouldn't be bringing up this level of emotion. This is a normal bag of Chex Mix, but in my hands, it seems weighty with meaning. He chose these for *me*. He remembered. I'm not much for showering men with praise for remembering simple things, but Wes is a different story. The Wes I met in that hotel room wouldn't have bothered using the brain-space for this. That version of him would have considered last night to be more than enough.

I hug the Chex Mix.

"Oh, my God, you're ridiculous." Hearing it out loud doesn't make it any less true.

His keys rattle in the doorway. How should I be standing? Next to the coffee table? In the kitchen, with some cookies on a tray, since we're apparently doing nice things for each other now? My heart flipflops in my chest. I drop the Chex Mix on the table, then pick it back up.

Wes cracks the door open and comes inside, bringing a burst of spring air with him. He looks a little drawn. I feel stupid, holding this bag, but now that he's inside, there's nothing to be done about it.

"Hey."

He drops his bag on the table. Our eyes meet, and his face lights up. I'm grinning like an idiot and I can't stop.

"That smile looks better on you than the tears," he says gruffly.

"It's highly offensive to tell a woman to smile," I shoot back, but I can't help it.

"I wasn't telling you to smile." He comes over to the coffee table and peers down at the candy. "I was only saying that you look nice this way. Your cheeks are all pink. You look happy."

Of course I do. Of *course* I do. "Someone was...very sweet to me. Was it you, or should I be concerned about breaking and entering? I know the security here is a joke."

Wes huffs a laugh. "It wouldn't surprise me if you had a secret admirer like that, but it was me."

"I take back what I said earlier. You're only fifty-percent asshole."

Wes's green eyes widen, and his gaze searches mine. What's he looking for? I mean every word. "What's the other fifty percent?"

"Hot."

He's more than *hot*. He's an inferno, the kind of tumbling heat that blocks out everything else, that makes me want to run straight into the center of the fire. I breathe in the scent of him. That Wes I dragged out of the hotel room—that wasn't the real Wes. *This* is the real Wes, which is green eyes sharpening with need, the sunflower streaks around his pupils expanding along with them. He's an asshole *sometimes,* but he's also a good man. I was right. Something was happening with him that day, and it made him different.

Jesus, I want him.

I wanted him last night, curled into the crook of his arm. I wanted him with every single breath. I wanted to kiss him, and I didn't want it to end at that kiss, didn't want to tear myself away at the end. The only thing I wanted to shred was the clothing between us.

He takes a deep breath. "I don't fuck around with roommates," he says, voice low, a challenge.

"Then don't fuck around." The urgency sweeps through me, glittering in my veins. It's been too long. I need someone. I need him. If I have to stand here, this close, for one more minute, all this need is going to burst out of me and make our apartment radioactive. "Just fuck me."

16

THE BAG of Chex Mix pops open between us, pretzels and cookie sticks falling to the floor. I don't care. I'm only reacting to a *very* reasonable request on her part. Request granted.

Whitney doesn't flinch at the sound of the bag bursting open or the rain of Chex Mix hitting the floor at our feet. It's like she's on the Titanic and I'm the last lifeboat—once I touch her, she's not letting go.

Her lips are soft and yielding against mine for the space of exactly one heartbeat, and then she growls deep in the back of her throat, her body working against mine. Fierce. That's the only word I can use to describe her in this moment. Fierce. It's as if all the grief and sadness from yesterday compressed itself down into the center of her and she's turned it into hot desire.

I know that feeling so fucking well, because I want her this much. The heat is equally as intense at the center of my spine, a coal mine of want compressed into something hard as diamonds.

"Wes—" She murmurs the word into my mouth, her lips making the shape of my name. It's so intimate it makes the hairs on the back of my neck stand up. Is she asking? Warning?

"Yes," I tell her firmly. I don't know what question I'm answering, but if this is the wrong answer, then fuck me.

It's the right answer.

We crash together again, Whitney nipping my bottom lip, and the teasing pain of it makes my cock jump. It's an incredible relief, the way she strips my mind of everything except her body, except the taste of her, her tongue battling with mine. She's nothing like the bubbly blondes I've picked up in bars around the world. Those women live in a pink cloud of whispers and shy smiles. Whitney might as well be prowling the jungle floor.

"Fuck," she says, sucking in a breath like there's not enough air.

I don't share that feeling. The air seems super-saturated, every inhalation making my vision sharper, my senses deeper. Whitney scrambles for the buttons on my shirt, her fingernails scratching through my undershirt as she claws at the buttons.

"I'll do it," I tell her, voice sharp, and it's not because I don't think she can do this. It's because I want to see her naked. I *have* to. "Take that off."

The buttons fly open underneath my fingers and I whip the shirt to the floor, followed by my undershirt. My belt is next, and I kick off my shoes. I'm in my boxers, nothing else, by the time Whitney stands barefoot in a ring of crushed pretzels. Her eyes are huge and dark, locked on mine, but she's struggling with the zipper at the back of her dress.

It's a navy thing, simple, clinging to her curves. Her face flushes pink. "I can't—"

"I've got it." I take her by the elbow and turn her so that her back is to me, shoulders rising and falling. The zipper is two inches down, caught on a loose thread. I run my fingers from her shoulder to her wrist just to see the goose bumps feather over her skin. "I want this dress off."

Whitney reaches to help me, and I catch her wrist in my hand. "Stand still," I tell her.

Standing still is hardly an option, but she manages it, even though she's trembling. I unhook the zipper from the thread and pull it down, opening her dress like the world's finest gift. She has a matching bra and panty set on underneath. Navy-colored lace.

Holy Christ.

"If you don't like it," she says softly, "then you're out of luck, because I'm not changing."

I spin her to face me and drink in the teasing, wanting smile playing across her lips. "You'd change, if I asked."

I'm not asking. I'm challenging. I can't help it. It's in the air between us, always. I'm only giving that tension words.

Whitney bites her lip and raises a hand to run her fingertips down the ridges of my abs. "If a man like you *demanded,* I'd probably have a more positive response." Her eyes flit up to mine and back down again. "I'm normally not into that kind of dynamic, but with you..." Her voice trails off and something flashes through her expression. There it is—that sadness. It's at bay, but barely.

I wrap my hand around the side of her neck and dip my face to the space between her jaw and her shoulder, kissing once, twice, three times. "I don't want you to wear different clothes."

"Good, because—"

"I want you to take these off. Right here. I want to see all of you."

Her eyes light and burn, the heat there morphing into a blaze. "Always about what the *men* want." She makes no move to slip a finger under the straps of her bra or hook a thumb into the waistband of her panties. "What if I want them on? What if I want to feel how—" I push a hand between her legs and press them apart. The navy lace panties are damp with her desire. "How—" I stroke two fingers over the fabric there, enough pressure to feel the outline of her beneath the ridges of the lace. Her lips drop open.

"Were you saying something?" On the last word, I yank those panties to the side and dip my fingers into the unbearably smooth, unbearably soft darkness between her legs.

Whitney sucks in a breath, probably struggling to find the perfect coy *but-what-if* response, but she's melting into my hands. "Nothing important." She gives a little pushback with her thighs, testing. I push them back apart and press my lips to her neck.

Her knees wobble.

No fucking joke.

A space in my chest that I thought would always be empty fills with a scorching wind. I want to push my fingers inside of her, I want to feel the way her body will open for me...

...but not here.

I take my hand away and lift her into my arms. She wraps her own arms around my neck and pulls herself up, so she can lick the line of my jaw. "Where are you taking us? Somewhere naughty?"

"A bed."

"What's wrong with the floor?"

Every breath is filled with her, every heartbeat is rocketing toward ecstasy. "I wouldn't want your knees to get sore."

We're in the bedroom in an instant. Mine, not hers. There are fewer distractions here. I know the soundscape of this room better than any other place in the apartment, and I want nothing in the world to take my attention from her body. I stand her on her feet at the side of my bed.

The light spills in from outside, tinged with spring, and makes her look golden and warm. Something to devour. Something to subdue. But there's a part of me that knows— I'll never contain that wild energy.

I can only try and bend it to my will.

"Take off your clothes."

In the stillness of the room, Whitney's eyes light up. She bites her lip. She shakes her head *no*.

"Then you've made your choice."

Her bra comes away easily, the straps silken under my fingers. The clasp falls open beneath my fingers. Her perfect round nipples rise in the cool air, beneath the swirls of my thumbs, and she arches back.

"Oh—" She breathes the word as my hands slide down the naked curves of her hips. My heart is in my throat at the warmth of her against my palms.

I push her backward onto the bed.

Whitney's eyes are wide, the dark lit in flashes of the sun, and I can't stop touching her. I can't tear my hands away from her face, her jaw, her neck. I need her skin against mine.

She bucks underneath me. "Here I am, naked in broad daylight, and you're still...partially clothed. How is that right? It's not right." Her voice is low and smooth and it makes the muscles in my back tense with anticipation. "It's not *right,* Wes."

I stand up and wrench the boxers to the floor. "That better?"

"Not better." Whitney reaches for me, and I tumble back into the bed.

Her arms go around my neck.

Her mouth is on mine, hot and wanting.

I push her backward to spread her out again, but she throws herself into my weight, twisting us so that I'm the one who lands on my back on the bed. She crawls over me, her body lithe and graceful, as if she's aware of every movement, and probably she is. That's how acting works. I half wish there was a camera to our right to capture every bit of light streaming over her curves, every touch of my hands against her hips, because I'd like to replay this moment for the rest of my life. Just so I can breathe.

She lowers her head to my collarbone and presses a heated kiss there, spreading her legs over the stiff rise of my cock. "You can't always be the one on top, Wes."

"Can't I?"

"No." Whitney rocks her hips forward and her wetness comes into contact with my crown. It's a like a shot going off, the beginning of a mission, and I'm bigger and stronger, so it's no contest when I flip us both, pinning her beneath me.

"I want to see you underneath me. I want to see the look on that pretty face the first time I take you, feel your body writhe while I show you how crazy you make me."

Whitney's eyes glow with the challenge. I don't know which of us moves first—do her hips rise or do mine thrust forward? All that matters, is that I sink into her, all the way to the hilt, and for the first time in a long time, I have the world in a firm grip.

17

WHITNEY

EVERY MUSCLE on this man is utter perfection. Utter provocation, if you ask me. One thrust of those perfect hips and I'm done for. He fills me with his eyes wide open, boring into mine, daring me to fuck him back.

What other option do I have?

What other option could I *want*?

I rake my fingernails across his back and he grits his teeth, then bends his head to kiss me so ferociously it's almost a bite. The pain twines itself around my pleasure and races down between my legs. Everything about him is pressure and my body fucking *loves* it. It gives me something to move against. It's like running into water—that resistance feels so good after living in the air for years and years.

"Let me—" I drive my palms into his chest and try to turn him over.

He presses his mouth into my collarbone, holding still. "Let you?" He growls the words into my ear. "What if I don't let you?" He draws himself in and out, in and out, his rhythm totally uninterrupted, totally under his control.

I wrap my arms around his neck and pull him closer, the frustration down at my navel curling into pure desire. "Why do I find that so *sexy*?"

Wes slows his pace and I tighten around him, trying my damndest to draw him in further. "So sexy, but you can't stop fighting me." He pulses inside me.

"You like it."

His eyes flash. "I can't get enough of it. Explain that."

"While we're fucking?" I struggle for a full breath. The pleasure is making me lightheaded, and I don't care. "You want to talk?"

"I'll listen to you." Fuck, he makes it look so *easy*, so nonchalant, even though I can tell from the tension he holds in his body that this is not easy, that this is something else entirely. "If you want to talk, I'll listen. Tell me again how much you love this."

I'm never into this kind of thing. I'm into men who worship me, who find me exotic and magical, and maybe Wes does too, but this isn't simple worship, a kiss on the back of my hand. It feels like desperate need, cloaked in something else.

I know all about that.

"I love it—" He comes in *deep* and it coaxes a sigh out of me. "I love it more than I thought I would."

"Oh?" There it is again, that little torque of his hips that rocks his crown against that rough, secret space inside me, and a moan slips from my mouth before I can cover it with my hand. "What about now?"

I can't look away from him. "More than most things."

Wes braces himself on his elbows, leans down, and licks my bottom lip. It's a slow, sensual motion in contrast with the unrelenting pounding of his hips. As soon as his tongue rises, he thrusts back in, so deep, *so deep*. "What about now?"

It's the perfect rhythm and every stroke is driving me toward release. I'm losing myself, breaking down around the relent-less beat of him, the heat spreading from my hips all the way to my fingertips, all the way to my toes. I can hardly breathe for the force of it. I grab for the sheets—anything to close my hands around—and Wes catches one hand, puts his own into it so I have to hold *him*. "What about now?"

It's blinding. "More than any—anything. I'm—"

Release comes like a wave, crashing over me even while Wes holds me in place. I have no choice but to bear my pleasure. My mind is all white light, Wes's green eyes the only thing to pierce through the haze. I'm a bundle of nerve-endings.

"Shit." He moves into me, filling me and stretching me, and I'm putty in his hands. I'm nothing, I'm weightless, so it is nothing for him to turn us both so I'm getting what I wanted after all.

Wes guides my hips with his hands, dragging me back and forth against him, and God, oh God, a second orgasm builds on the tail of the first. I plant my palms against his chest. "Oh, no." My voice sounds far away. "I can't. I can't—"

"You can. I want to see it happen. I want to watch your face."

Heat blooms across my cheeks but there's no other option, and I don't want another option. I sway my hips from side to side to test the strength of his hands and they are *strong*, they are solid, I couldn't get away even if I wanted to.

I throw my head back and my hair comes loose from the knot at the base of my neck. Wes makes a sound low in his throat when it happens and his muscles work between my legs.

It hits.

The sound I make is half-animal, half-desire, and so encompassing that all I can do is hold on for dear life, my hands on his chest. His grip on my hips is the only thing keeping me upright. I feel him flex, feel his legs tense, as he digs his feet into the mattress.

"Look at me."

I do.

He comes hard, his face lit up in relief and release, and I find it within myself to rock against him, even though I am a puddle. I am jelly.

The last moment of his climax comes and I feel it, sense it, and watch it trail away into the past. Then I slump to the bed beside him, panting.

"You're glowing." He follows it with a chuckle.

I laugh out loud and shove him a little with my fingertips. "I'm sweating like a pig. That was a *workout*."

"Oh, please," he scoffs. "I did all the work."

"All the work? I—" I'm ready to argue, but Wes pushes

himself up on one elbow and kisses me. It's still hard, still strong, still Wes, but there's a backdrop of gentleness that makes my wounded heart flutter.

He pulls back. "Better not do that."

"Why not?"

"We might end up in bed all day."

"Oh. Right." I muster as serious an expression as I can. "That would be a tragedy like the world has never seen."

He stretches, muscles gleaming in the shaft of sunlight coming through the window, and rolls over me, his weight only a whisper against the rise of my breasts. Wes jumps to the side of the bed and stands up, stretching again.

I'm suffused with energy. He's fucked the sadness hangover right out of me, but watching him stand there—what is he *doing*?

"Do you...have plans?"

Wes leans languidly against the doorframe. "You don't? It's Friday night." He runs his hands through his hair, taming the mess that I made. "Don't you usually go out with your friends?"

It stings, somewhere beneath my skin, the fact that he's pushing me into leaving. I throw off the covers and swipe my clothes up into my hands. "Yeah. Sometimes I do."

"Whit." He blocks my path on the way to the door. "You're..." He laughs. "You're scowling."

I try to push past, but he's faster, bigger. "I'm going out.

Friday night." I put on a fake smile and remember to let it go all the way to my eyes. *Acting.*

He raises a hand to my chin and tilts my face up to his. "Don't be an ass."

My mouth drops open. "*I'm* the one who's not supposed to be an ass? You're hustling me out the door after—"

"I am *not* hustling you out the door. I'm trying to find out, in the least pathetic way possible, if you're free tonight." Wes presses his lips into a thin line. "To go out with me."

"I thought you didn't date roommates." I can't keep the smile off my face.

He runs a thumb over my chin. "We're past that now." He straightens up, dropping his hand. "Unless you'd rather pretend this didn't happen."

"We *should* pretend this didn't happen. You're not my type."

Wes steps into my space and the nearness of him heats the air. "I'm *not*?"

"No. Not at all."

"That's not what it sounded like when you were moaning *I love it more than anything.*"

"You have a perfect dick," I tell him solemnly. "I *did* love it more than anything."

"In the past tense?"

I shrug one shoulder. "Who's to say? There is only now, and the present is an ever-changing—"

He sweeps me up into his arms, my breasts brushing against the hard surface of his chest, and kisses me. *Fuck*, it's hot. It's that confidence, that control, that gets under my skin, into my bones. I part my lips for him to let his tongue in to do battle with mine. He backs us up until the backs of my knees are pressed against the side of the bed, and I squirm in his arms. I'm pinned, but I like it. It's so opposite of what I normally want, but I need it.

He pulls away. "Are you really going to tease me like that?"

His lips are perfect too. I can't stop looking at them. "If that's what it takes."

"What if we have dinner instead?"

I reach down between us and grab his thickness, already hard and standing out from his carved, luscious body. "Fuck me one more time, and then we can go to dinner."

"Isn't that the opposite of how things are supposed to—"

I drop my clothes, put my hands on his shoulders, and twist until he falls back onto the bed. I'm on him in an instant, hips rocking.

I hear no more complaints.

18

"Don't say it."

Whitney pauses with her mouth half-open on the tail end of a sentence that started with, "I definitely think we should go to," and I'm not going to that place. That wine bar. No.

"Vino."

I pull a t-shirt over my head and make a face at her. "Is that the only place you like in the whole city?"

She crosses her arms, which has the effect of pushing her breasts up into a positively salacious position. "Of course it's not the only place that I like. It's my *favorite* place."

It helps that she's wearing a brand-new bra and panty set, close to the ones I took off of her an hour and a half ago. It took that long to tear myself away from her body and get us both into the shower. It was either that or fall into her eyes forever, and I can't do that.

I don't know why, but I can't do that.

She's not making it easy.

"I have a different favorite place."

My entire body is loose, relaxed. I raise my hand to my neck to rub at the ache there, but there's no ache.

There's...no ache.

"What's your other favorite place?" Her voice cuts into my revelation. It draws me back to her. She's an enigma. She's her own source of gravity.

I drag a finger down from the hollow of her neck to the warm, scented cleavage rising out of her bra. "Here."

Whitney puts a hand on mine and presses it closer. "Stay a while."

"Oh, my God. Are you sex-obsessed?"

She gives me a serious expression. "Maybe. It's a possibility. But the only way to find out is..." She hooks an answering finger in the collar of my shirt and tugs me closer. My head spins. I put my hand on hers and meet her with a kiss.

"Are you trying to kill me?"

"Not right now." Whitney leans in for another kiss.

It's a fine line with her, like it is with hard liquor. Being inside her, *taking* her like that, melted the tension out of my shoulders and my back. It stripped my guard away. But if I lean into it too far, it comes back. There's a resistance at the base of my spine that I can't abandon. I don't know what's on the other side.

"You're going to, if you keep this up." I keep my tone light, but she pulls back, her dark eyes searching mine.

A smile quirks the corner of her lips. "Ah. I get it. You're too hungry to go on."

It's half-true. I'm hungry enough that my stomach is an empty pit, but I can feel that edge, feel that line between relaxation and losing control creeping forward. It shouldn't be. This is Whitney. This is supposed to be fun. But it's like going out for a drink and knocking seven back. The cure's the same for both—food, and something more like conversation.

"Is it that obvious?"

"Men are always ravenous."

I push her away from me, getting some distance. The sweet soapy ocean scent of her body wash is tantalizing, and I need a breath of air, or else I'll fall headfirst.

Maybe I already have.

"Get dressed before I take you back to bed."

Whitney turns away, swinging her hips on the way to the door. "Don't tempt me."

"I am *not* tempting you."

She drags her fingers along the edge of my dresser, the fuchsia bra and panty set caressing her skin. My pulse pounds in my temples. If she doesn't get out soon, we're going to be in major trouble. We're both going to be in over our heads, and I don't even know what this is supposed to *be*. I have no idea what outcome Whitney's hoping for.

I don't know what outcome *I'm* hoping for.

The tips of her fingers knock against my phone, sending it

spinning across to the corner. "Oh—sorry." She stills it with her hand and it buzzes against the wooden surface of the dresser. "Somebody's sending you a message." Then, as if it's the most natural thing in the world, she flips it over in her hand and steps back into the room. "Who's Bennett Powell?"

The name coming out of her mouth is a jolt. I shake off the sensation that she's somehow violated my privacy—and really, who the hell cares?—and take the phone from her hand. "My missing roommate."

Her eyes fly open. "Oh, my God." Whitney dashes for the bedroom door and runs across to her own room on the balls of her feet, like a gazelle, fucking graceful, like she's just been caught out in the woods. "Yeah, you're right. We *have* to go to dinner. A missing roommate? What other secrets have you been hiding?"

~

WHITNEY INSISTS on choosing a restaurant at random.

I feel it right away—that tightening at the base of my neck, my shoulders drawing up. Maybe she was right. Maybe we should have stayed in bed for the rest of the night. For the rest of the weekend, even. It's been a long time since that knot loosened at all. I *was* used to it. Now it nags at me.

We walk side by side down the street by Whitney's favorite place in the early evening glow. I rub at my neck.

"Miss me already?" Whitney jokes, then puts her own hand on the back of my neck. It's a foreign feeling, her fingertips there, but I shove down the impulse to push her away.

"You didn't do anything sexy to the back of my neck."

"Yet."

"You're something else. You know that?"

"I've been told. What about here?" She gestures to a Thai place with a menu posted in the window. It looks like people have been picking at the edges. This Week's Menu is scrawled at the top, along with a date from six months ago.

"Not a chance."

Whitney sighs. "Have you no sense of adventure?"

"I have a sense that I'd rather not get food poisoning."

I turn down three more restaurants, the pressure in my neck growing, until finally Whitney stops outside an authentic Mexican place. It's a building wedged between two others, about as wide as an alley, and colored lights spill out from the front windows and the doorway. *People* spill out from the front, coming and going. The place is packed. It's loud as hell. *No.* I don't want loud, or people.

In the street behind us, a car screeches like it's dying. It's a metal-on-metal whine and it burrows into my brain, a flash of pain at the base of my neck, and my heart zig-zags against my ribcage.

"Wes?"

Whitney has stepped in front of me, toward the two low steps of the restaurant. She holds the handle of her purse lightly, as if she's never once heard of being robbed in New York City, and her eyebrows are raised.

I missed something, but I don't know what.

I move toward her, putting myself between the purse and a

group of women stumbling out of the restaurant, arms linked, screeching with laughter.

"Any objections?"

I have a thousand objections, but if I keep saying no, then Whitney is going to choose on her own. And the longer we keep walking, the better the odds that she'll choose somewhere truly outrageous. It's Friday night in New York City and things are only going to get rowdier. I'm bracing for the inevitable collision in the traffic several beats before I realize it.

"This place." I give it a nod like it was my idea all along, and stride toward the doorway, sweeping her up in my arm as I go.

Our booth for two is tucked into a little arched alcove, and I twist in my seat, looking for the exits. We're twenty feet away from the door in the kitchen, which isn't bad, though the front door is—

"What are you looking for?"

"Exits." I snap back to Whitney's face before I can come up with a convincing lie.

"Exits? For the building?" She peeks out over one of the menus, which has a colorful sombrero on the front. My stomach growls.

"Old habit."

"Military thing?"

I pick up a menu and force myself to focus on it. "What, you don't look for the exits every place you go?"

She arches one eyebrow. "Not usually?"

"You're just asking to get trapped if something goes south, you know."

"Okay. So it *is* a military thing."

"Not necessarily." I scan the left side of the menu, and then the right. "I was friends with Dayton growing up. You know that."

"What does that have to do with finding the exits?"

I get a quick little film reel of all the stupid shit Dayton and I used to do as kids, and later teenagers. It was like being drunk, in a way. I never had a reason for anything, other than the adrenaline rush that came from skirting the edge of risk.

Or diving right into it.

"You wouldn't get it. You were probably a rule-follower."

A veiled hurt flashes in Whitney's eyes. "Not exactly."

That was the line, and I blundered right into it like a self-absorbed asshole. I take her hand. "Hey." Her eyes flick to mine over the top of the menu. "I know you're not some goody-two-shoes—"

Whitney snorts. "I think you're the first person to say that in a hundred years."

"—Mary Sue, prim and proper—"

She covers her mouth with her other hand and grins.

"—stuck-up—"

"Too far, too far…"

"—uptown girl."

She bursts out laughing. "No. None of those things." She slips her hand from mine, not unkindly, and jabs a finger at me. "You should count your lucky stars that I'm not."

"Why?" I lean in close. "Because of the sex?"

"Because of the room you sleep in—"

"I don't always *sleep* in there."

"—in my apartment."

"I'm paying half the rent."

"Oh, but I had to *choose* you. I wouldn't let just any man move in with me."

"No." A bright truth, like a camera flash, goes off in my chest. "Just a control-freak veteran in need of a roommate."

Whitney slaps her menu to the table and claps her hands. "That's the magic word."

"Veteran?"

"Roommate. Tell me about your missing roommate."

As if on cue, my phone buzzes in my pocket.

I didn't answer the first text.

Now there are two.

BENNETT: Hey

BENNETT: You ever coming home???

"HE'S MISSING," I say bluntly.

Whitney nods like a therapist. "Mm-hmm. Yes. What can you tell me about *why* he's missing?"

I put the phone face-down on the table. "Bennett Powell walked away from Newark a while ago. Maybe three months? Three-and-a-half, now that I've been in the city. I looked for him, but it seemed like he didn't want to be found. And now—"

The phone buzzes again.

"—now he's texting me. Out of nowhere."

Whitney reaches for the phone. I pin it down with my fingertips. "What are you doing?"

"Answering him. I'd bet a hundred dollars you haven't said a word."

"How would you know that?"

"Because you haven't typed anything in. Did he show up at your old doorstep? That's so *mysterious*." Her face is contemplative, shining. "What's he like? Why would he walk away?"

I can't picture his face—not the way he looked in Newark, when we were sharing the two-bedroom in a brand-new development that overlooked a parking lot. I signed the lease on the place before I was officially out of the Army. I still waffled about it every time I picked up the pen. But it came back to me—that tank. The crunch of the metal. The unholy screech.

One week later, Bennett Powell was knocking on my door.

"I don't know. Maybe he was looking for something."

I can't resist it. I turn the phone over.

Bennett: I'm waiting outside, Wes.

I show it to Whitney, and her eyes go wide at the words on the screen. "Seems like now he's looking for you."

My stomach turns over. "I don't want to be found."

19

WHITNEY

"I'VE BEEN THINKING."

Wes doesn't stir. He's deeply asleep, on his side, his back to me. His shoulders rise with every breath. Not a single hitch at the sound of my voice—nothing.

It *is* six in the morning. The weekend sunlight at the end of May is a hazy yellow, the color blooming from the morning gray. That light, playing over his skin, makes me want to tackle him, wake him up with a biting kiss, but I'm not that much of an idiot.

I've been awake for a while.

All I learned from Wes at dinner was that Bennett Powell, his roommate, walked away from Newark for three months. Wouldn't answer calls. Wouldn't answer texts. He sent one cryptic message and got out of town. Or somewhere else in town.

It's been on my mind ever since.

The weekend's free, with nice weather and sunshine, and

Newark isn't *that* far. The desire to shake things up is so strong I can't shake it out with dancing, or improv class, or pretending I'm on set while I'm selling insurance.

Hence why I've showered and packed a small bag, intending to make this a road trip for the ages. At least as far as Newark.

I try again. "Wes."

He takes in a sharp breath and rolls over, muscles glorious in the dawn light. "Whit—what are you doing in here?"

"I've been thinking."

He flips onto his back and throws an arm over his eyes. "Why don't you think quietly in your own bedroom?"

"We're stuck in a rut. We need to *do* something. We need to get out of town."

Wes pushes himself up on one elbow and looks at me. "You're free to leave town any time you like."

"I want you to go with me."

I've caught his interest, but he narrows his eyes, his hair adorably sleep-flattened. "You're as transparent as Saran Wrap. You know that?"

"I am not. I am opaque. I am the very model of mystique."

"You want to go to Newark and find my missing roommate."

"Fine—maybe I am transparent." I rock forward onto the balls of my feet and back down again. "But, look. When's the last time you took a trip for the hell of it? When's the last time you did something spontaneous?"

"When I moved in here with you. That was pretty spontaneous. And now you're waking me up at an indecent hour to—"

"I know you get up early on the weekends, Wes. You're only missing"—I glance at the clock on his bedside table —"ninety minutes of sleep." I run over to the bed and perch on the edge. "Isn't that worth it? If the trade-off is excitement? *Adventure?*"

"Trust me. Newark is not an adventure."

"I could make it an adventure." He wraps an arm around my back, curling into me as if by habit. "Come on. Trust me."

Wes looks at me, his eyes glinting in the dim light.

Then he climbs out of bed.

∾

WES: Where are you?

His text comes in exactly fifteen minutes after he steps into the shower, all thanks to me. I want to jump him. I've wanted to jump him every day since last Friday, but it's as if the air between us has turned solid. I can still sit next to him, I can still talk to him, I can even still *touch* him—but Wes seems to have doubled down on the kind of disciplined life that makes me want to burst out of my own skin.

There's the gym membership, for one thing.

I text him back.

Whitney: Outside—waiting by the car.

On Sunday morning, he went out and came back four hours

later, his hair damp and his shoulders relaxed. I'd leaned against the kitchen counter, casually pretending that I hadn't spent the last four hours trying to burn off the incredible energy of wondering. I'd gone running. I'd watched three episodes of a new reality show on Netflix. I'd *made tea.*

"I got a gym membership," he'd announced into the air while I stirred the sugar into it.

"You look like it," I'd practically purred.

But he'd only flashed that smile at me and asked if I wanted to grab lunch.

Wes: Be right down.

Wes jogs down the steps of the front entrance three minutes later and plants his feet in the center of the sidewalk, a little duffel bag slung over his shoulder. "Clothes for a weekend, in case," I'd shouted at him from outside the bathroom door. He heard me.

"You entrapped me."

I toss him the keys. "If entrapment is the same as renting a car, then yes, I entrapped you."

He jiggles the keys in his hand and stays put. "There's no way you planned this all this morning."

"Fine. I put in for the car rental last night with an absurdly early drop-off time. But if you really don't want to go…"

I'm provoking him, and I know it. But he's been so distant, so *uptight,* this week that I can't help but think…

Well, I think a lot of things. And those things are best discussed on the open road.

Wes takes a deep breath of the fresh, clean morning air, brimming with possibility. "Are you dead set on going to Newark?"

"No. But I think you are."

He laughs out loud, the sound echoing off the front of our building. "I am *not*."

"I hate to appeal to your military sensibilities—"

"Then don't."

"—but isn't there a saying that goes 'Never leave a man behind'?"

He rolls his eyes, his mouth curved in a smirk. "Powell left *me* behind." A bird calls into the beat of silence. "But you have a point."

I clap my hands together. "Yes, I do. I was right all along. Come on—let's beat the traffic out of here."

"I'm driving."

"Yeah." I shoot him a look and open the passenger-side door. "You're holding the keys."

"This isn't going to be much of a road trip." Wes steps on the brake, bringing us to a smooth stop at the first stoplight after our apartment.

"No?"

"Newark is thirty-five minutes from here, this early in the morning."

"Right. I looked that up last night too." I tip my phone into my purse and wedge it between my foot and the center console of the car. The pressure there reminds me of Wes's hands on my hips, and my mouth waters at the memory of it. "We can keep driving."

He cuts a glance at me. "I thought you were set on going to Newark."

"Is your friend Bennett Powell an early riser?"

"I have no idea. He got up early when we lived together, but it's been months since then. Maybe he's changed his ways."

"It's going to be eight in the morning when we get there. If we go straight there."

"Is there somewhere else you want to go?"

"You tell me."

Wes sighs. "I'm not that kind of guy."

"You're not the kind of guy who picks up and goes to destinations unknown?"

We roll forward through the intersection. "Not usually."

"So about last weekend—"

"My God, woman."

"Was that an unknown destination?"

"You entrapped me," he says again. "You entrapped me to have some weird conversation about the fact that we had sex one time—"

"It was more than one time. And you *loved* it. So why the deep freeze?"

"Deep freeze? Is that what this looks like to you?"

We pass by a Chinese restaurant snugged up next to a Sephora. I could spend an hour in there, changing everything about my face for the hell of it.

"It feels like it." I make a hammering motion that looks one-hundred percent absurd. "And I want to smash it."

He sighs. "You've been waiting all week for this." It's not a question.

"Well, yeah." I can't look him in the eye, because he's driving. I wanted it this way for him, but I'm regretting it now. I look out the windshield. Peeking at him out of the corner of my eye is awkward as hell. But twisting to stare at him seems worse, in a way. I settle for the middle distance of the dashboard. "Listen, I know I...pushed."

"Pushed *me*?"

I think of those words rolling off my tongue, as if it were a scene from a movie. *Fuck me*, I'd told him, and he did. He did exactly as I asked. "I'm the one who initiated our...encounter."

"I'd agree with that assessment. But it wasn't unwelcome."

Wes delivers this news in such a flat, matter-of-fact tone that it takes a few beats for me to register his meaning. "Wait—it *wasn't* unwelcome?"

"Jesus, Whit, have you seen yourself in the mirror? Of *course* it was welcome. And it's not only that. You've got this unbelievable—" He holds the steering wheel tight in his hands. "You drive me crazy."

"Is that a good thing or a bad thing?"

"Both."

I breathe in the silence, waiting for him to fill in the yawning blank.

It goes on a *little* too long—another stoplight—for him to speak again.

"It's good in that you're irresistible. But it's bad in that..." Wes's voice trails off.

"You're killing me."

"I'm used to order." He looks at the road, turning carefully onto the side street that's going to take us to the highway out of the city. "I'm used to some level of control in my life. You're the opposite of that."

"But it's irresistible. You *need* that, on some level."

"I need something," Wes admits. "But you didn't hear me say that."

TEN MINUTES OUTSIDE NEWARK, the urge to speak boils over.

"Don't hate me."

Wes groans. "I loved it, okay? I admit it fully. What we did last weekend was dangerous, but it was awesome too."

"Whoa. Don't get in over your head, fella."

He shoots me a look as we glide over the freeway, hovering right at the speed limit. "I can feel you over there, you know. Getting *in over your head.*"

"Fine." I lay both hands flat over my chest. "Your body has taken me over. Your moves in the bedroom have consumed me. And Wes?"

"Yes?" He wears at least a half-smile. I can see it from here.

"I know this isn't the kind of thing that's supposed to work out."

He laughs. "What makes you think that?"

"They say that opposites attract. Nobody ever talks about what happens when they collide."

We whip past a road sign—four miles to go. "It gets awkward," he says. "People pull away from each other."

"But what if *people* don't want that to happen?"

"Hypothetically, they could give it a shot." He cuts a glance at me, a strange hope burning in his eyes. "Even though, hypothetically, it could be the mistake of a lifetime."

"We all make mistakes," I say diplomatically. "Plus, you've already crossed the line."

"What line?"

"Not fucking around with roommates."

"Tell me. What loophole did you find, Whit?"

I clear my throat like a fancy professor. "It's not fucking around if we give this a serious try. Just to see what happens." Every inch of me tingles with excitement, with anticipation. It steals the breath from my lungs. It's brighter than the rising sun. I know I'm pushing too far. I know I'm pushing too hard. But I need him close to me. I need the wall to come back down.

"Deal."

I take his hand in mine, yanking it clean off the steering wheel, and kiss the back of his knuckles. I know it's a risk. And I don't care.

"You gonna let me drive?"

"Yeah. Drive wherever you want." I let go of his hand, but my palms ache to take it back. "The world is your oyster."

"You're the one who wanted to find Bennett."

"Right—yes. Let's find your missing roommate, and then let's get a room."

20

"WHERE SHOULD WE GO FIRST?" Whitney furrows her brow and watches the high-rises of downtown Newark go by in the bright morning sun. It's not long until June, and part of me is desperate—*desperate*—to see Whitney in one of those fifties-style bathing suits, laying out on the beach. "You don't think Bennett is still waiting at your apartment, do you?"

"He'll have found somewhere else to go."

"Did you text him back?"

"No."

I see her head swivel toward me out of the corner of my eye. "Are you going to?"

"Not right now."

She waits a beat. "Why not?"

"Because I'm starving." I steer us onto a side road. Three blocks in, there's a diner with an honest-to-God parking lot. "You dragged me out of the apartment before I could eat."

"Where's your spirit of adventure?"

"I'm *on* the adventure. But a man can't travel on air alone."

"You should embroider that onto a throw pillow."

I pull the car into the parking lot and turn it off with a decisive flick of my wrist. "I'm not embroidering anything. But I will order breakfast for you, if you want."

"You're so *manly*." She says it lightly, a joke, as she's leaning for the door handle, but I catch her wrist. She spins back to me, eyes aglow.

"Am I going to have to remind you how manly I am?"

Whitney's face lights up, her cheeks turning pink. "That sounds *filthy*."

"You said you wanted to give this a serious try."

"And I meant it." Her chest rises and falls with shallow breaths.

"If you're serious, you know you can't always be in charge."

She bites her lip. "I am *not* into men like you, but damn, Wes..."

I rest my fingertips at the curve of her jaw, then drag them lightly down the side of her neck, her shoulder...and back to where I held her wrist. Then I take my hand away. Whitney sucks in a breath, like the loss of contact is as palpable as a shock. "You hungry?"

"Ravenous." She flicks her eyes down to the front of my pants, where there's an obvious bulge. "And you look like you're—"

"Ready to go." I throw open the car door and step out. "Come on. Let's go get a table."

Whitney lets out a frustrated grumble. She follows me anyway.

"Does your neck hurt?"

I pull my hand away and look back at the wreckage of breakfast on my plate. I'm on the edge of eating too much, so there's still a third of a pancake left, but I put my fork down several minutes ago and settled for coffee. The old habit must have taken over.

"No."

Whitney narrows her eyes. "That's not the first time I've seen you rub your neck like that." She wraps her own hand around a mug with the diner's logo in white. She ordered half-coffee, half-hot chocolate, which seems exactly like her. "Did something happen? You know, while you were in the Army?"

"Yes. I broke my neck."

Her eyes go wide.

"I'm kidding. No. Nothing happened."

She blows a breath out through her lips. "Getting blown up isn't *nothing*, Wes."

"My sister can't keep her mouth shut, can she?"

"In her defense—" Whitney takes a deep sip of her drink and closes her eyes, as if mediocre diner coffee and hot chocolate from a package are the nectar of the gods. "She was talking about Dayton, not you. You just happened to be part of the story."

I stare down into my own coffee. The heat curls up around my face, but when it makes contact, it's not the humidity of a hot drink but the dry heat of the desert. The pedal presses hard against my foot. It takes force to steer the Humvee, it takes strength, it takes a steady hand on the wheel and a confident stomp of the boot. It's not some zippy rental car, and the road isn't the recently patchworked highway between New York and Newark. It's dirt and stone, deep tracks pitted into the earth, and the Humvee dips and bounces over each ridge.

"Wes?"

"Yeah?"

Whitney's face is the picture of concern. "You've been looking at your coffee for"—she glances at the clock behind the counter—"several minutes." She draws her bottom lip between her teeth. "Did I say something wrong?"

Something unhinges in my chest, a valve releasing, and I want to tell her. I want to tell her everything. How that Humvee haunts my dreams. How I find myself in the driver's seat every time there's a fender-bender in traffic. How looking at Dayton—my best friend, even though I don't deserve him—leaves me feeling sick inside.

But I hesitate.

She's out of her comfort zone already and in the back of my mind, I hear a warning. Telling her, as much as I want to, is the third rail.

"What made you come to Newark, anyway?"

There's the truth at the very base of it. A woman. Julie. We met one weekend on base, and she was moving there. It didn't work out. But even so, I thought I could hide from everything in Newark—from the memories. From the guilt.

I couldn't.

The waitress buzzes by the table and drops the bill neatly between us. "Can I get anything else for you two?" Whitney reaches for the bill and the waitress winks at her. "Oh, honey, let him pay. Look at him! He's got *you* out the morning after. That must count for something."

Whit flashes her a smile I recognize from her audition practices and nods, her nose wrinkling. It's almost too cute.

The moment shatters. I press my lips shut tight. A woman like Whitney—*especially* Whitney—doesn't need to hear about the things that happened when I was thousands of miles away. All that might as well have happened on another planet. It has nothing to do with her.

"She's right." I snatch the bill off the surface of the table and dig for my wallet. "I'll get this one."

"Aren't you *manly*?" Whitney flutters her eyelashes, but I see right through the little joke. I'm not going to get out of this. Not forever.

"Okay. Here we go." Whitney claps her hands in the passenger seat of the rental car. "I'm belted in. Let's find your roommate."

"We can try, but no promises. He's the kind of guy who doesn't always answer texts."

"So...exactly like you."

"I'm answering right now."

Whitney grabs my wrist. "Is this too much? Did I—" She purses her lips. "Did he leave on bad terms? Am I pushing you back into a bad situation?"

I pause, my thumbs above the screen. "The situation was that he left. I got one text that said he had to hit the road and asked if I wanted to meet up later."

"It wasn't a cry for help, was it?"

"Whit, I looked for him around town. Either he didn't want to be found or he was somewhere else entirely. I'm betting on the latter."

She tips her head back against the headrest. "This could be *so* awkward." Then she pops up again, eyes alight. "I'm kind of living for this."

"I can see that."

I tap out a text to Bennett.

Wes: I'm in town. Where are you?

"There. I sent it."

We both stare down at the phone, waiting for a reply.

Traffic whooshes by on the side street. The knot in the back of my neck tightens. I'm not paying attention. I'm trying not to pay attention.

"Well." Whitney taps her fingers on the dashboard. "Looks like he's not going to—"

The phone buzzes in my hand.

Bennett: Branch Brook. What took you so long? Do you have a spare key?

∾

"Wow." Whitney puts her fingertips to the car window. "This is too precious for my withered heart."

I laugh, my heart in my throat. "Withered heart? I don't think so."

The Cherry Blossom Welcome Center *is* almost sickeningly delightful, and I scored a good spot in the parking lot. We get out of the car and Whitney takes a deep breath of the air. "Sweet. Like springtime."

The welcome center is surrounded by lawns, neatly tended, and paved pathways. When I look back at Whitney, she's already gone, trotting across the parking lot to a sign with the park map on it.

"This place is *huge*." She glances over her shoulder at me. "Oh, good, it's you."

"Who else would it be?"

"It's busy here." She squints at the map. "Did he say where he might be? Otherwise, we could spend all day here and never cross paths. The paths *do* cross, over here, but it's far enough that—"

"You really left me hanging there, Sullivan."

I'd recognize that voice anywhere.

I turn to face Bennett Powell. "Do you always sneak up on people like that? Where the hell did you come from, anyway?"

He gestures vaguely at a path on the other side of the lot. "I've been walking. Where have *you* been? And who's this?" He has a lazy grin that I find equal parts infuriating and familiar.

Whitney moves gracefully around me and sticks out her hand to shake. "Whitney Coalport. We've been looking for you."

"Is that so? Wes, is she telling the truth?"

Bennett Powell does not look like the military man who sat in the backseat of that Humvee. He looks like a college student, with tanned skin, a faded t-shirt, and unruly hair. He's got a knapsack slung over one shoulder that does look Army-issue, but if it weren't for the telltale perfect posture, I wouldn't have guessed he spent any time in the service.

"Yeah. We drove over because she thinks you're some kind of lost puppy."

"Lost puppy." His eyes flick from me to Whitney, and I can see him sizing us up. I edge closer to her, trying to make the movement look natural. "I can see that." He shifts his weight from side to side and tilts his face up toward the sun. "You guys want to take a lap around the short trail while we talk?"

"You guys go ahead." Whitney puts a comforting hand on my arm. "I'm going to check on the welcome center and practice for my audition next week. Meet up in a bit? I'll be around here."

I'm seized with the urge to grab her and devour her like I'll never see her again, but I settle for a neat kiss on the temple.

There. Now Powell knows we're together.

"Sounds good. See you soon."

Whitney gives a little wave and pulls her phone out of her pocket, putting it to her ear. Then she turns lightly on her feet and heads for the welcome center, stopping to look at a baby in a stroller on the way.

Powell interrupts the pang in my chest. "Let's go, man."

He heads for one of the trails, but I move toward a different one until he's got no choice but to follow.

"I'M GUESSING there's no spare key," he says, looking up at the cherry trees. There are a few late-as-hell blossoms on the branches, but most of the petals cover the ground, flattened by people walking over the greenery. "When did you leave?"

"About a month ago. I got a job in the city, and rush hour's a bitch."

Powell grins at me. "Whatever happened to bros before—"

"Shut your mouth, man."

He hikes the knapsack up onto his arm and sticks his left hand in his pocket. "She's gorgeous, man. Why didn't you say something?"

I stare at him. "First, it's—" I don't have to explain myself to him, but I feel a tug at the center of my chest. "It's new. We live together."

"Already?"

"She had a spare room, and I needed one. So, to answer your question, there's no key. I broke the lease on the place, since there was nobody to cover the rent."

"It was a nice place," Powell says thoughtfully. "The commute was really that bad?"

I hate how he looks at me, those searching gazes with bright blue eyes. It makes me feel like I have something to hide.

"Yes."

He waits. I don't answer.

"I've been doing some research." Powell's footsteps are gentle on the path. Not heavy, like boots. "About that mission."

"What's done is done."

"It's not done, though, is it? It's not done for me." He stops in the middle of the trail, and I follow him.

"It's over, Powell. There's nothing to learn about it. It happened, and we survived, and it's over."

"I disagree." He leans in close. "Don't you ever think about it? Don't you remember how—"

There's a rush of blood to the head, a pounding in my heart, and I hold up both hands. "Listen. I'm glad you're doing okay. I packed up your clothes and had them sent to your mom's house, so anything you're missing should be—" The back of my neck tightens in tandem with the ache at the base of my spine. "I've got to get back. If you need anything else, you've got my number."

I turn back the way we came, walking fast along the trail, back to the welcome center.

"Sullivan," Powell calls, but I don't answer.

21

"WHAT HAPPENED?"

Wes shuts the door with a stony expression and jogs around the front of the car, practically leaping into the driver's seat. He stares straight ahead as he turns the key in the ignition, then turns his head with precise movements to look behind him.

He backs out of the spot.

He accelerates forward.

He still hasn't spoken.

That's not entirely true—he burst into the welcome center a few minutes ago like a man on a mission. His eyes had zeroed in on me like lasers. "Let's go."

I almost had to break into a run to keep up with him on the way to the car.

"Wes? What happened?"

He lets out a deep breath and smiles; a slow, deliberate thing that rings a warning bell in the back of my mind. "He wanted to get into it with me about the past."

"Get into it with you? What'd you do, steal his girl?"

He laughs out loud, but there's a sharp edge to the sound. "Just shit that happened while we were overseas. I'm not interested in dwelling on it." Wes turns right out of the park entrance and we cruise down the street, heading back to the taller buildings at the heart of downtown Newark. "I told him what he needed to know. And then I left."

"What'd he have to say about that?"

"I didn't stay to find out." He turns down a side street into a residential neighborhood, seemingly at random. "Anyway, wish granted."

"Wish *not* granted. I wanted to learn more about your mysterious disappearing roommate, and you left him behind, in a park filled with fallen cherry blossoms. Is this the beginning of a fantasy novel or what?"

Wes pulls up to a four-way stop and grins at me. "Listen to me. The morning is young. It's ten o'clock. We have two full days before we have to be back to work." His smile falters, and he braces himself, as if this is an enormous personal risk he's taking.

For all I know, maybe it is. "What's your point?"

"You said the world was my oyster. I take that to mean I have the freedom to drive this rental wherever the hell I please."

"You do," I admit. "But what about the thrill of the chase? What about letting the wind take us wherever it may? What about pointing at a map and choosing at random, and—"

"Have you ever been to Connecticut?"

"No. Wait. Maybe." I close my eyes. "Maybe when I was younger? I can't remember."

"Have you ever been to Chester?"

"I don't think so."

"Then let me ask you this. Do you like castles?"

"This is patently unfair. You want to visit a place you've already been? That's hardly adventurous, Wes. We could go anywhere, and you want to go—"

"To someplace we've never been *together*."

I glare at him.

"Are we giving this a serious try or what?"

My chest swells with joy at the thought of it. I keep slipping into those old habits—of being an adversary, of being on the other side of an invisible wall. Wes has turned us both and faced us bodily in the same direction. "Does that mean I have to go along with your plans?"

"Yes. Sometimes it means that you have to let me choose our destination."

"But there's a castle."

"Jesus, Whit. I wouldn't lie about a castle."

"Okay. On one condit—"

A car behind us honks and I jump, my hand flying into a one-fingered gesture as Wes, unfazed, accelerates through the intersection. "No conditions," he says. "This one's mine."

He cuts his gaze at me when he says it, as though it's not really the trip he's talking about.

"Look up."

I've been shading my eyes with my hand, looking out over the little waves making diamonds on the surface of the Connecticut River, until Wes's simple command breaks me out of that reverie.

I look where he's pointing.

There, rising out of the trees on the mountain, is a castle.

I gasp so loud it could be mistaken for a theater affectation, and clap my hands over my mouth. "Holy shit! You weren't kidding."

"I was absolutely not kidding. Wait until you see the inside."

"I don't think I can wait. I think I'm going to jump off this ferry and swim." It sounds ridiculous, but my entire body is lit up at the sight of the strange stonework shape of it. It's nothing like the collection of clapboard houses in every little Connecticut village we've driven through so far, including the one we passed through to board the ferry.

Now I see why Wes insisted on coming this way instead of driving straight there.

There's a modern-day ferry rumbling beneath us, the big motor vibrating through every piece, but I have the breathtaking sensation of being drawn into a mystical past. The kind of past where anything could still happen, and anyone could still be alive.

"That would be highly inappropriate."

"I'm highly inappropriate most of the time."

Wes locks his arm around my waist and pulls me close. My body sighs at the solid weight of him next to me. "So I've noticed."

"I thought of something horrible."

He pushes me away a few inches to look into my eyes. "You're going to bring up horrible stuff on the way to see a *castle*?"

"Just once. Before we actually get there. Unless you want me to hold it inside, eating away at the core of me until—"

"Tell me right now. Quick. We're almost there."

"We have to tell Summer."

Wes gapes at me. "My sister, Summer? You want to call her up and tell her about coming to a state park in Connecticut together?"

"My *best friend*, Summer, who is also your sister, yes." I look him straight in his heart-stopping eyes. "We should tell her we're dating. Can you imagine how awkward it would be if she came over for dinner and deduced it for herself?"

"Is she coming over for dinner?"

"We don't have any plans yet, but—"

"Then let's not worry about it."

WES HANGS BACK from the tour group, looking up toward the

balcony railings around the second floor in what I'm delighted to discover is called the "Great Hall." It's essentially an enormous living room, if that living room were perched right in the middle of a mansion disguised as a castle. The tour guide, a lovely woman with black hair in a sharp bob, points out the architectural features.

But all I can see is Wes.

He pulls his gaze down from the top of the room and back to me. "You're *beaming.*"

I put a hand over my mouth. "I can't help it."

He takes my hand and twines his fingers through mine. "You like this place that much?"

"It's—" It's like a set piece. It's like a dream. Some guy with an imagination as whimsical as mine decided to build a *castle,* and this was the end result. A collision of Medieval stonework and American fantasy. "I love it."

"And you haven't heard about the doors yet."

As if on cue, the tour guide steps out into the middle of the group. "Gillette Castle has forty-seven doors, and no two are the same." She has a twinkle in her eye, and I have a flickering vision of her dressed in a medieval outfit, sweeping through the halls at night. It's all absurd, since we're standing in what was essentially a private home built in 1919 in Connecticut, but there's a heavy magic that's settled over me since the moment the ferry docked. "Each door is its own puzzle, with secret mechanisms that make unlocking them a test for Gillette's brightest visitors."

I squeeze Wes's hand. "Forty-seven different doors?" I can't express in words how much I love this idea. How much I love the idea of forty-seven unique puzzles, all leading to different spaces, inside one house.

"That's the coolest thing about it," he murmurs into my ear, tugging me close.

"You like that the best? I wouldn't have pinned you for a unique-door guy. More of a new-build guy. Where every-thing is fresh off the assembly line and matchy-matchy."

Wes shakes his head. "If I built a house, it wouldn't be one of those prefab things. It would be..." He laughs, softly, so as not to interrupt the tour guide. "It wouldn't be *this* crazy, but there would be elements."

Something sparks in the back of my mind. The Wes I know wouldn't build a house with this much variety, with this many puzzles. Houses like this have a mind of their own. Was he not always like this? I file it away to ask Summer about later.

Upstairs, there's a stonework balcony overlooking the Connecticut River, and I pull out my phone. "Smile. I want a picture."

"Are you serious?" Wes runs a hand over his hair, which is completely unnecessary, as he keeps his hair neatly trimmed and groomed *always*. "This is what you want a picture of?"

"I want a picture of your face, with mine, looking like we want to be here." I turn my head and kiss his cheek. "Looking like we're giving this a serious try."

Wes gives a fake sigh of disapproval, but then he wraps his arm around my waist, pulling me in close. I lean my head against him. The picture on the screen tugs at my heart—

there he is, grinning widely, not a hint of the serious, self-contained man I know.

And there's me, leaning against him like I can trust him to be there for me.

Like I can trust myself not to push him away.

The thought is like a distant clap of thunder, too far off to worry about now, but there nonetheless.

I stick my phone into my pocket and look out over the river. "We can't stay here, can we?"

"In the castle?" Wes wraps his arms around me and rests his chin on my shoulder. "No. Not tonight."

"You say that like staying here is a possibility."

"There are ways. Groups can stay here, I think. I read about it in the paper once."

"What paper? How did you find out about this place?" I twist around and put my hands on either side of his face. "Are you secretly from here?" I put on my most solemn, serious face. "Wes. Tell me the truth. Are you the secret owner of this castle?"

The grin drops from his face, and he looks into my eyes, eyebrows raised like I've stumbled upon a secret.

"Whit, there's something I have to tell you." My heart leaps into my throat. Visions race through my mind of somehow being the lady of this weird-ass castle in the middle of America, of having sex with Wes in every single room, of graciously entertaining tour groups passing through. It'd be like throwing my current life, with my audition rejections and insurance sales, right into the river, never to be seen again.

"Wes," I breathe. "Are you serious?"

He looks deep into my eyes. "No."

I burst out laughing, a mix of relief and disappointment, and slap halfheartedly at his shoulder. "You ass. You had me going."

"You're the one who went there in the first place," he says. "Come on." He puts an arm around my waist and we go back through the castle, out onto the green lawns. "Do you really think I'd forget to tell you about something like this?"

"You keep things under lock and key. That's for sure." I rise up on my tiptoes to kiss his cheek. "But I'll get them out of you. Just wait."

22

———

WES

WE CHOOSE our bed and breakfast through outright humor. Whitney laughs so hard at the name *Bee and Thistle* when I read it from a list off my phone that tears come to her eyes. "Oh, God, we *have* to get a room there. Please tell me there's a room there."

It might be a cutesy coastal place with a cutesy name, but they have a room available, and that's what matters.

We stand at the doorway to our room and Whitney squares her shoulders. "Are you sure you're ready to take this step?"

I give her a look. "What step?"

"Sleeping together. On vacation."

A frisson of nervousness runs up my spine, but I dismiss it. "Yes. But first, we need to get lunch."

"You and your food." She pushes the door to the room open. "Is that all you ever think—oh."

The room is dominated by a huge four-poster bed, each of the posts carved from dark, polished wood. It's piled high with throw pillows, but the massive frame looks sturdy enough to hold the two of us.

It looks sturdy enough to bend her over it.

We've been so close today that my body is aching with the need to be closer. Until this moment, I was ready to remain in total control, ready to insist that we have a chaste stroll downtown to a little cafe, but the heat in Whitney's eyes has me thinking far filthier thoughts.

Her eyes find mine, dark like the posts of the bed, dark like my thoughts, and she steps close, her hands wrapping around my shirt like she's trying to throw me off-balance.

"Wes. Do you see this bed?"

"I see it."

"How hungry are you?"

I let my duffel bag fall to the floor and toss Whitney's over-sized purse on top of it. Then I lift her into my arms, her sundress spreading open as her legs go around my waist, and walk us both into the room. I kick the door shut behind me and it closes with a soft *click*.

"Let's find out."

Our clothes fly away like they were never meant to be worn, and Whitney crawls up onto the bed, her ass bobbing pleasantly in the air as she throws one pillow after the other to the floor. There are still more than enough left when I catch her wrist in my hand. A shiver runs through her at my touch that makes my cock harder than steel.

"You're messing up the room."

She bites her lip. "So what if I am? What are you going to do about it?"

I lean down and kiss her, using her momentary stillness to turn her onto her back and spread her wide over the comforter. "Stop you."

"Oh, are you? I don't see how you could. I am, after all, a grown woman and quite strong for someone—"

I cup my hand around her jaw, raising her chin a fraction of an inch. She arches her back, her nipples standing out against her breasts, and I feel it there, holding her in my hand like this—a need. A raw need. I can't put it all together, not with my cock aching for her body and my mind drowning in her eyes, but I know, instinctively, that it must fit mine. God, please, let it fit mine.

"Be silent." I say the words with all the authority I learned in the field, in the Army. I say it at the same volume I'd have said anything then, if we were pinned down, if a single shout of command would have blown our cover.

Whitney opens her mouth and closes it again.

"That's a good girl."

I wait for her to roll her eyes.

Instead, she spreads her legs another inch. I can't tell if she means to do it or if it's a reflex, but it doesn't matter.

"What if I'm *not* good?"

To her credit, Whitney whispers, but I let my eyes linger on hers while I drag the pad of one finger down to her breasts, circling one nipple at a time, and then lower, over her navel, and lower. It's painfully intimate—my body hums with it—and my skin prickles with the vast difference between fucking her last weekend and fucking her now. Last weekend was an act of desperation. This is an act of intention.

"You can't help yourself, can you?" Her cheeks are rosy. "You want to be good, but you can't allow it." I dip two fingers between her legs and swirl them through the hot wetness there.

"I don't know if I can or not." Whitney's eyes flicker away from mine, then back or not.

"Let's find out."

She wriggles beneath my hand, her hips swaying from side to side, and the color in her cheeks deepens. "You know, I might not be the best person to get so *deep* like this—"

"Deep?" I push two fingers inside and flutter the outside of her clit with my thumb. "We've only scratched the surface." I bend to kiss her, to taste her, and she makes a little noise into my mouth that's totally at odds with the bright, too-loud Whitney I know. When I pull away, she tries to follow, picking her head up off the floral-patterned comforter, but I push her back with a hand on her chest.

"Be good."

That shiver—that trembling, running from shoulders to hips.

"Okay," she whispers, then presses her lips closed.

I lean down so that my breath brushes the pink shell of her ear. "Put your hands above your head. On the post there."

She does.

I take a deep breath and go exploring.

I run my hands over every inch of her—the soft skin at the undersides of her breasts, the flat of her stomach, the curves of her hips. I press her legs apart, wide, so she's on display for me, and check that her hands are still on the post.

They are. "Good girl."

She's wet and pink and pliant in my hands, and I lower my face to the slick folds between her legs.

Jesus, she tastes good.

One stroke of my tongue after another and Whitney isn't silent, but she's trying her damndest, making little *mmm mmm mmm* noises in the back of her throat. Edging against the rules. It's technically not speaking, though she freezes when I take my tongue away from her pussy. Her hands still grip the post of the bed, white-knuckled, her breathing fast.

"Good girl," I say again, then return to the feast.

She starts to come apart at the seams when I pay special attention to her clit, sucking it into my mouth, swirling it with my tongue, and her hips lift from the bed, rocking against my face. There is no pain at the back of my neck, no pressure over my shoulders. I could stay here forever, if the need to fuck her didn't grow stronger with every passing moment.

"Oh—"

Whitney tumbles over the edge into release, her hips bucking, and I slip three fingers into her wetness just to feel her muscles work. My cock pulses in answer. I don't stop until she shudders and relaxes, panting.

There's a moment when I have a sinking disappointment that somehow, I've fucked this up, somehow, she's going to be satisfied with this moment. I push myself up to my knees and wipe at my mouth with the back of my hand.

Her eyes follow my movement, lock onto mine.

A glittering heat flashes through those dark eyes.

Then Whitney—slowly, deliberately—takes her hands off the post of the bed.

"Who said you could do that?" I move up to nip at her bottom lip, letting her taste herself lingering there.

"I broke the rules," she says softly, breaking another in the process. "I did the wrong thing." Her voice shakes, and my chest struggles to contain the feeling welling there. It's so powerful I want to put a hand to my heart. Like standing underneath a cathedral bell while it rings. She's asking me for something. No pretense. No performance. We are not pretending to be roommates, we're not pretending to dip our toes into the shallow end of a relationship. She's stripped bare in more ways than one, and like a lightning bolt, I know what she needs.

I put my hand on the side of her face and rub my hand across the blush of her cheek. "You did the wrong thing," I echo, and I watch her eyelashes flutter closed for a hot second before she meets my eyes again, the skin beneath my thumb going scarlet. "But I forgive you."

She sucks in a sharp breath and arches, her energy filling the room like radio static, like the rush of a waterfall, and I dig my fingers into her hips to hold her in place. "Fuck," she says. "Fuck." Then it's a whirlwind of arms around my neck, of hips pressing against mine, a fevered pressure. Whitney is insatiable, uncontrollable, and I let her turn me onto my back and straddle me, her pussy angled above my cock, so close I can feel her heat.

"How about this?" She plants her hands in the center of my chest and rocks her hips, teasing, tantalizing. "Is this good?"

I have my hands on her hips, so I feel every movement beneath my palms. I look her straight in the eye, straight into that vivid darkness. "So good."

"No, it's not." Whitney grins, wicked and wild. "It's torture, waiting."

She doesn't make me wait any longer.

We come together with such force that it squeezes the breath from her lungs. I pin those gorgeous hips down and rise up into her, lose myself in the curve of her neck as she throws her head back, in the half-moon pain of her nails digging into my chest. She rides me with complete abandon. She rides me with so much abandon that I have to rein her in, pull her to my chest, and kiss her, swallow her moans and cries with mine, so we don't get kicked out of this too-cute bed and breakfast.

She urges me on with her hips, with her tight pulses around my length, and it's so *Whitney,* so fucking timeless. I can see her anywhere, any time, running ahead, looking back to wave me on, always running, always choosing a different direction, zigzagging across space like some kind of electric butterfly, unpredictable and breathtaking all at once.

When she makes me come, I see the stars.

THERE'S a deep silence in the room for a moment, the blood rushing through my ears. It recedes slowly, and other sounds cut in—birds singing in a tree outside our window. Footsteps on the stairs in the hall. Whitney's even breathing.

I roll over to see if she's asleep and she sits up, a strange smile on her face.

"Christ. I thought you were sleeping."

"Sleep?" She stretches her arms above her head. "How could anyone sleep after a thing like that?"

"People all around the world could sleep after that. *Billions* of them, even." There's a satisfied heaviness in all my limbs, but I push myself up on one elbow anyway. Whitney hops out of bed, arms still stretched into the air, and does a slow twirl.

"Not me." She won't look me in the eye.

"I can see that." I let myself rest against the pillow, breathing in the scent of her on the blanket. She moves across the room in long strides to where our bags are piled on the floor, picks hers up, and digs through it.

"We didn't lock the door." She flips the lock and laughs. "That would have been so awkward for someone else to walk into."

I don't want to get up, but the energy has shifted, and while Whitney rifles through her purse, I follow her out of the bed. She flicks her eyes to me and blushes.

"Hey."

"Yeah?"

Instead of asking the question, instead of saying the words out loud, I pluck her bag from her hands and fold her into my arms. I hold her tight. And then I tilt her face up toward mine and kiss her like I'm giving this a real, honest-to-God try. Because I am.

How could I not be? How could I see her like that, open to me in every way possible, and not try, even if the risk is a terrible one?

Whitney relaxes, the tension going out of her. When we come up for air, she puts her fingertips to her lips.

"Everything's okay," I tell her.

She nods. "Except one thing. Well, two things."

"What are those things?" I stroke my hand lazily down her back and relish the feeling of her leaning into me.

"For one thing, we need a shower."

"You look so wicked when you say that."

"I didn't say it *only* needed to be for cleanliness purposes."

"Is that the second thing?" I shouldn't want more of her, but I do. Blood rushes down from my head to my nether regions in an instant.

"No. Lunch is the second thing." Whitney closes her eyes, as if in rapture. "Food. To put in our mouths, to savor, for food is the only—"

"Enough talk," I tell her sternly. "Let's go."

She laughs all the way to the shower.

But I can't leave it at that. I turn those laughs into moans, using only my fingers and mouth.

That'll show her.

23

"ARE YOU FREE TONIGHT?" Christy's voice sounds breathless, like she's walking fast down a sidewalk in the city. She probably is.

"Are you asking me out on a date?" I lean back in my chair at the insurance agency and pat at the elegant bun I've twisted my hair into this fine morning. "It's not like you to make last-minute plans, but—"

"I've got an audition for you, Whit." She steamrolls me with the excited confidence only an agent can pretend to have. "I know it's last-minute, so if you turn it down, I'll understand. But it's also something out of the norm."

"Like a Viagra commercial?" I've done auditions for tens of commercials—hundreds, even—and most of them involve wearing scrubs and smiling into the camera while holding a clipboard. "Slinky red dress?"

The guessing isn't half-hearted out of defeat so much as an aching nostalgia. I *miss* last weekend with Wes like I miss some of the better Christmases of my childhood. I want to be back on that balcony with him, at that strange American castle. It wasn't called a castle when it was originally built. I learned that much from the tour guide. It was only the man's home.

"You still there?"

Christy didn't hear my Viagra joke. I sit up straight in my chair. "I'm here. What kind of audition is it?"

She says something that's muffled by a cacophony that highly resembles traffic.

"I didn't catch that, Chris. What did you say?"

"It's for the stage. Off-Broadway."

I burst out laughing. "Are you shitting me?"

"I'm not kidding. It's a cool role. You could be good for it. I convinced them you had the chops. Seven?"

"I'll be there."

"I'll text you the address."

"—YOU'LL be paired with Jason, who's cast for the romantic lead. We're still working out the understudies. I'm sure you know how that is."

The director, Rowan, doesn't look up from where she's scribbling on a notepad.

Me? I'm center stage, in the middle of jumbled set pieces that seem to be standing in for someone's vision of a living room. It's hot under the lights, and they're bright as hell.

Jason sits on a stool made from two milk crates stacked together, flipping through the script.

"Do you mind if we switch places?"

Rowan looks up at me over her glasses. "Excuse me?"

"I'd like to switch places with Jason."

His mouth quirks in a smile. I throw Rowan the most confident expression of my entire lifetime. Her eyebrows lift. Is she impressed or annoyed? It doesn't matter, in the end. She'll remember me.

My heart pounds, but I coolly look down at the script, like I'm just working out the final details. Like I've had it far longer than the fifteen minutes I've been staring at the pages, trying to make the words shuffle themselves into a discernible order. Christy met me outside the theater, shoved the packet into my hands, and left, still on the phone.

"Switch places with her, Jason."

He stands up from his crate-stool and gives me a subtle nod on the way to my spot on the stage. There's another reason for this, too—I want Rowan to see my good side. In these ridiculously bright lights, I'm going to need every advantage. She can't spend the entire audition looking at the way my nose looks weird from that angle.

"Take it from the top. Page thirty," calls Rowan.

I take a deep breath. The house lights are up, which reminds me of theater class back in high school. All those practices, and when those damn lights finally went down, you could find yourself in another world. No such luxury. Not this time. I have to find myself in another world right now, three feet away from Jason, in the middle of a Goodwill junkyard.

It's not a walk in the park, either. This isn't the giddy meet-cute at the beginning of the play, where our characters first meet. This is the heartbreak at the center of the show. I can feel it, even though I haven't read the entire script.

"You good?" Jason gives me the grace of one final moment to collect myself.

"Let's do it."

His face transforms. That's the only way I can think to describe it. One moment, his expression is neutral, positive even, and the next, it's darkly seething. The set pieces around us fade out, becoming an apartment in my peripheral vision. I feel her—I feel the character I'm supposed to be playing settle in over my skin, feel her rage, feel the subtle way it shapes my face—jaw jutted, on the verge of angry tears.

"I've had enough," growls Jason. "Do you ever think of anything but yourself?"

"Me?" I jab my fingers into my own chest, flicking my eyes down to be sure I've got the lines. "You have no idea what I've done for you. You have no idea—"

"Say that again." He storms toward me, and I plant my feet. "Say it to my face."

"I will say it to your face, because it's true. Look at me. Look at me when I say it."

He inches closer, and the chemistry between us crackles in the air. "How?" His hand comes up to the downstage side of my neck, a featherlight touch that will look like a grab from the first row. "Like this? Is this how you want it?"

"*Yes.*" I deliver the line with all the thunder I've ever stored in my chest, all the hope and hurt locked away for my days at the insurance agency. "That's how I want it, damn you, that's how I want it." The script falls to the floor of the stage. My hands, I find, are wrapped around the front of his shirt.

He leans in, closer and closer, and then—

"Thank you so much, Whitney." Rowan's voice is a clear cut across the heat of the scene, and all at once, the weight of Jason's fingers on my neck reads differently. Outside the scene, it's all wrong for a man to be touching me there. Outside the scene, I want to run from the theater and straight into Wes's arms.

He'll be at home, waiting for me. Waiting to hear all about it.

Jason and I break apart.

"Great job," he says, wearing an encouraging smile. "That was really good."

"Thanks." The adrenaline spikes again then, glittering in my veins, the rush that comes from nailing an audition. And I *did* nail it. I absolutely did. I beam out at Rowan. "Thanks so much."

"We'll get back with you," she says, scribbling more notes on her notepad.

I grab my purse and stroll out through the theater, taking deep breaths to cleanse myself of the dangerous excitement pulsing through me. *Damn,* my hopes are high. It would be icing on the cake, really, to finally land a role. This thing with Wes—this risky, tentative, serious thing—is enough to make all those hours at the agency seem like nothing.

But getting this?

This would be a godsend. I'd *finally* have a success to tell Summer about. The four of us could all go out together and talk about how our dreams were coming true.

I walk through the dusky evening light. I should call her. I should call her and tell her everything. It's her brother, after all.

If I get the part, I'll tell her. That's what I'll do. It'll be a surprise. Everyone will be so surprised and happy for me, especially Wes.

I catch the train home with his name on my lips.

24

"—so we're going to need to scrap this part of the project and rebuild from the ground up. A total pivot."

Greg's voice cuts through the desert heat drying my brain from the inside out in time for me to register that I'm being fucked over. I flip the topmost page on my folio and try to wrench my thoughts into some kind of order, out of the sunburned anger flaring up from the center of my chest.

"That's—" It's bullshit, is what it is. I've been managing the living hell out of this project—an in-house surveillance plan for a client out in the suburbs—for two weeks.

Two weeks I've spent with my mind still at Gillette Castle. That place could be a fortress. I can't get the wide, green lawns out of my head, or the view from that balcony. Up above the river like that, you could see trouble coming. You could make the walls thick and sturdy and lock the doors, and never encounter a fucking crane again in your life.

"Wes, you're the best person to run point on that, since

you're our person on the ground. We'll need to start with the internals first and move on to the—"

"No."

Greg looks up from his notes, eyebrows slightly raised. I should back down. I should be deferential. He's my boss. But he's being a fucking prick in this moment, and I can feel the dust storm particles against my skin, the tearing metal from the crane I walked by on the way to work this morning still ringing in my ears.

I grab the last remaining shred of control with both hands and force myself back into order. "I'll look at the internals, but the externals need to be set in stone first. If we're scrapping everything, I want my people to go about it in the right order." I deliver this news in a tone so nonchalant that there's no possible way it betrays my fury at being blindsided.

Greg gives me a slow nod. "It's client feedback behind this push. This is not a referendum on your work."

Around the table, the other project managers shift in their seats. Part of me, deep down, wants to lower my head, wants to slouch my shoulders and sheepishly apologize for causing a scene. But my heart beats in a sick off-rhythm and there it is, the crunch of the Humvee tires on the gravel road, and fuck that. Fuck that, if I'll ever apologize for asserting myself. It's what got me out of Afghanistan and back here alive. Back here to sit at this meeting and watch as Greg reshuffles everything I've been devoting my time to.

I put a smile—or at least a neutral expression—on my face, and let myself lean back an inch into my chair. "Of course not."

"Just so you know." Greg cracks a smile. Crisis averted. For him, anyway. I need to wash the grit off my hands, out of my eyes. I need to get home to Whitney. She'll make me feel clean. She'll make me feel like there are a thousand miles between us and the rest of the world. I know she will.

WHITNEY FLINGS OPEN the door before I can put my keys in the lock. "*Wes.*" She sings my name, her voice pitched high with joy, and throws her arms over her head. "You're home. *Finally.* God, I'm into you." She leaps at me, her arms wrapping tight around my neck, and plants a lipsticked kiss on the side of my neck, then another square on the mouth. It arrests the forward motion I was committed to in the hallway.

Get inside.

I have to get inside.

"Aren't you going to ask me why I'm in such a good mood?" Her dark eyes glow and she bites her bottom lip, rosy with her lipstick. Whit rocks her weight backward, tugging me along with it, and for the life of me, I can't find her rhythm. All I want is to be inside.

I drop a hand to her waist and pull her close. "I don't have to ask that. It's because I'm home." Another thought rises to the top of my consciousness. "You're here early."

She takes a deep breath, as if to scream, and the muscles at my core brace for the piercing sound. "Igotapart." The words are a breathless jumble. She's trying to contain herself, but it's not working very well.

"Tell me again, in English."

"I. Got. A. Part." Whitney beams at me, and I take her all in —the little black dress she'd never wear to work. Her hair, sleekly arranged in a twist that's made for nightlife. The words coming out of her sweet mouth. "A part, Wes. I got a *role*. I'm officially cast in an off-Broadway show." She's incandescent with joy.

"That's amazing," I say, because that's what you're supposed to say when you're the boyfriend of an actress. This could be Whitney's big break. She's been talking about this audition for a straight week now. I should have seen it coming. "Let's go inside and celebrate."

"Go inside?" She waggles a finger at me. "We're not going inside. We're going out." She takes my hands in hers. "This calls for a real celebration. Jesus, Wes, I have so much to tell you. I can't deliver this news on the same old couch from our old life."

My head throbs, and I pull her in close, trying to get her to stand still. "Are you sure about that? There are other things we could do to make the celebration—"

"It's dinner or nothing." She puts her hands on either side of my face and pulls me in for a kiss that starts out chastely happy and deepens into something racy and dark, and I'm split in two. I would do anything for Whitney. I would say anything for Whitney. But that pain in the back of my neck is spreading up onto the top of my skull and more than anything, I want to throw the deadbolts on the door behind us. The apartment is a far cry from Gillette Castle, with miles of quiet space surrounding it, but at least we can be inside our own walls.

"I'll cook anything you want. Say the word."

"No cooking," Whitney demands. "We're going out. I'm *sure* it's been a long day at work. God knows it's been hellish for me, having to sit through staff meetings when I had news like this to tell you. There's so *much* I have to tell you, Wes. It's going to be insane." She puts her palms to the top of her head like there's no possible way she can hold all the thoughts in. "We can't possibly cook. Let's go. Come on. Change your shirt and let's go."

Whitney leaps back toward the door and grabs her purse from inside. The words rise to the tip of my tongue—*I'd rather celebrate at home*—but I swallow them down. I can't bear the thought of her face falling. I can't bear the thought of taking any of her joy from her, as much as the outside world grates on me.

A few minutes inside. I'll take a few minutes inside, and then I'll be fine. It will all be fine.

"I'll be right out. Okay? Just let me change my shirt."

"I'll be right here." Whit swings her purse up onto her shoulder and leans against the wall, as sultry and vibrant as she's ever been. It rips my heart in two. "Waiting for my favorite man."

"—NIGHTS during rehearsal. The schedule is kind of crazy, but that's okay, right? You'll have plenty of time to revel in solitude."

"What?" It's unbearably loud in Vino, which apparently doubles as some kind of dance club on evenings when I don't want to be out. They've got the music cranked to such a high volume that it's hard to focus on the words coming out of Whitney's mouth, despite the fact that her red lipstick highlights every movement of her lips. Desire punches its way up through the haze in my chest. I want to kiss her. But I can't hold on to the feeling because of that fucking music. "Sorry. I can't—" I motion around my head.

Whitney tips her head back and laughs, shimmying her shoulders. "I know. It's so violently loud. But it makes me feel *alive*. Or maybe it's the wine. Probably all of it. God, this is such a good day." The next moment, she's out of her seat, around at my side of the table. "Dance with me."

"Christ, no. There are limits."

"Come on. Dance with me."

She tugs on my hand. I don't stand. A body that's sitting would rather be sitting. "Whit—"

"I can't hear you," she says over the music and pulls hard enough that I stand.

"This isn't that kind of—"

"The hell it's not." Whitney swings her hips on the way to a dance floor—an honest-to-God dance floor—crammed against the opposite side of Vino. I slow down, taking over the pace, and she shimmies up to me, laughing, her hands on my waist. "See? Dancing."

There are two other couples on the dance floor, all of them obsessed with each other. I want to sink into the moment, to let Whitney show me what that's like, but I can't.

I can't.

I'm apart from it.

She's snugged right up against me. The only thing separating us is our clothes. But she's on the other side of an impassable divide. I want to lock a door—any door—behind us and tear the fabric away.

My head throbs.

I take Whitney's hand in mine and spin her out, then back in, the tension easing now that I'm the one leading. I learned how to dance at a program my mom put on at her school, a thousand years ago and a million miles away.

Whitney is beside herself. "I didn't know you could dance."

"False. We danced together at my sister's reception."

"I didn't know you could dance like *this*."

It was less urgent, at the reception. I wasn't trying to tame her then. No—that's not the right word. I wasn't trying to contain her then. Tonight, it's a different story.

She moves faster, throwing herself headlong into the moment, ratcheting up the energy on the dance floor. It's seductive as hell, the way she moves those hips, but I don't want to be seeing them *here*. My mind won't shut off, and that urgent need to be somewhere away from the open, away from being a viable target, buzzes down my skin like a razor.

I catch her on the next spin and she twirls right into me, against my chest.

"Let's go."

"Are you kidding?" She turns in my arms and somehow

manages to execute the movement so gracefully, it looks like a legitimate dance move. "We've only had one glass."

"Let's *go*."

"Oooh." Her dark eyes light up at the gravel of my voice. "I like you when you're like this."

"Not likely." I curve my arm around her waist regardless. For once, she comes around without a fight.

I drop too much money on the table—a more-than-generous tip—and Whitney protests. The music echoes in my ears. "It's fine. We're celebrating, remember?"

She blushes, furiously happy, and chatters all the way back to the apartment.

I slam the door behind us and flip the locks, then lean my forehead against the cool wood.

"Wes? You okay?" She sounds far away, but she's only standing in the middle of the living room.

"Long day." It's true. It's been a long fucking day. It's been a long several years, and some of those years won't leave me the hell alone.

"Come to bed," she says wickedly.

It's nearly an hour later when she curls up against my chest, panting, her cheeks flushed, the little wisps at her hairline curled from the heat. I've never been so tired. Not since I was overseas. Every one of my limbs is heavy, weighted down, and Whitney's body curled against mine anchors me to the bed.

She sighs happily. "We should enjoy this."

I'm struggling to stay awake, but this rings a warning bell in the back of my mind. "Why? Aren't we already enjoying it?"

"Things are going to be so crazy, now that I have this role." She shrugs her shoulders, settling in. "Who knows when it'll ever settle down?"

25

"Why do we wait *so long* to do this?" Eva throws her arms around my neck in the afternoon version of Vino. "You look so happy. Did you land yourself something amazing?"

Joy bubbles up in my chest like champagne bubbles. "More than one thing."

"Sit, sit." She gestures at the table. "I've already got celebratory wine. Let's lift our glasses before you tell me the good news."

We do, and I laugh out loud. "It's not as good as your news. You're killing it, Eva. And so humble too!"

She blushes. Eva, for her part, never once mentioned that she *had* a new release, much less that it hit the *New York Times* bestseller list. I found out via an ad I saw on one of my social media apps. And we even *texted* about this meetup fairly extensively.

"I hate saying it out loud." She takes a sip of wine, eyes

darting around as if she's vaguely nervous that someone might approach her in Vino based on her book jacket photo. "It seems so—" She wrinkles her nose. "I don't know. Braggy."

"In that case, I have no good news."

"Oh, stop. Tell me yours. Immediately. I demand it." Her eyes sparkle in a genuine kind of way that reminds me of Summer. I'll call her right after this. I'll invite her to dinner. How can she refuse? She and Dayton are deep in the thick of parenthood, but everyone needs a night out once in a while. Plus, Wes and I have yet to debut our relationship to them. My heart zigs and then zags against my ribcage. It's going to be awkward—no two ways about it. Across the table, Eva looks at me with wide, prompting eyes. What better time to practice?

"There's...more than one thing, actually." I sip my wine and try to look coy, but it slips down the wrong pipe. I try to clear it, but I can't swallow it. Commence coughing fit. "There's —" More coughing.

"You okay?" Eva's brows are knitted together with concern, but her mouth is quirked, like she knows in her soul that I'm not *really* choking on wine. "It's okay if you'd rather keep it to yourself."

It makes me laugh, which brings on more coughing. She's doing her best to keep from laughing, one hand over her mouth, but there's a light in her eyes like there used to be in high school, when we spent all our time backstage whispering naughty jokes and generally being nerds.

"Not funny," I wheeze.

Eva arranges her face into something resembling serious-ness and waits while I catch my breath.

"Should we consider this a sign that your good news is meant to be secret?"

"Please. You're the one who hides all your accolades." I bravely lift the wine glass to my lips and take another sip. "If I were you, I'd take out a billboard. Do something crazy."

"That's *your* thing. Doing something crazy just for the hell of it." She's right, but a little spark of pain shivers through the center of my heart. I dismiss it, like I always do. "Now, tell me your news before we get old."

"I got a role." I watch her face as it sinks in. God, she's genuine. The joy lighting up her expression doesn't hold a hint of jealousy. "It's off-Broadway, but that's okay, because I think a Broadway show might be too demanding for my new boyfriend."

"*What*?" Reserved, adult Eva slaps her hand down on the surface of the table. "Good God. Why didn't you lead with that? Who is it? Who? I want names."

"That's the crazy part." I feel breathless to speak this out loud. "It's Wes."

"Roommate Wes?"

"The very same one."

She blinks at me, wordless.

"I know. It makes...little to no sense." I take a sip of my wine, successfully this time, and relish the bubbly heat of it as it slips down my throat. "He is *not* my type. Not in any way, shape, or form."

"Oh, stop." Eva waves a hand in the air. "I saw the picture. At the very least, he'd be any woman's type in *form*."

It makes me laugh. It borders on a giggle, and that's a little much, so I pull it back. "That's right—you called him sexy man meat the last time you were here. I've come to discover that it's a *very* accurate description."

"So what's the hang-up?"

I shrug my shoulders, gazing into the space between us, visions of Wes's naked, muscled body dancing like perverted sugarplums in my head. "I'm not sure that it's a hang-up, so much as it's—"

I'm lost for words, because my dirty thoughts have slipped down to the V at that hard lower edge of his abs. *Bring it back, Whit. Back to your longtime friend who has graciously met you at Vino for a girls' evening out in the middle of the most hectic scheduling of your entire life.* "I don't know. Maybe it's an 'opposites attract' kind of thing. I've learned a hell of a lot more about him than I knew before."

"As in, he's not just a one-dimensional asshole?"

That side of Wes had softened, the rough, defensive edges of him smoothing. Slightly. "He can still be an asshole. *Everyone* can be an asshole sometimes." It flashes up into my memory then, as clearly as if it were yesterday, shouting at my father and storming away. I can feel the shape of the words in my mouth. I swallow more wine to chase them away. "He likes to be in control."

Eva frowns. "How controlling? Be honest with me." I can see the concern lighting like a signal fire in her face.

"No, not like that. *Not* like that. He just—he has a plan, and he likes to stick to it. He's not the kind of guy who thrives on surprises."

"Oooh." She murmurs the word into her wine glass, one eyebrow arched. "And this is fireworks instead of fizzle?"

"He takes me from day to *night*."

"Seductive. But how does he...live with you?" Eva guffaws, a completely unladylike sound. "How does he stand it? I mean that in the nicest way possible."

"I've grown out of my former erratic ways. I've got a job. Two jobs. *And*. I keep the spontaneous road trips under control. I've only woken him up early on the weekend once."

"Yes, that all sounds *incredibly* tame. I'm sure he'll love those late nights at the theater."

"Hey, bitch, I say this fondly, but are you trying to rain on my parade?"

Eva laughs until tears gather at the corners of her eyes. "No! No. I'm sorry. It's a terrible habit. I spend too much time writing about people and not enough time drinking with them. Clearly. It makes me morbidly curious."

"I'd be curious too. Have you seen my boyfriend?"

We laugh for another hour, until the wine has gone thoroughly to my head.

IN MY HEAD, I'm in the middle of a breakup scene. In reality, I'm trying to sell a man insurance.

It's not going well.

"This isn't going to work for us," I hear myself saying, and sit upright with a jolt. Hollywood's Man of the Year looks disapprovingly down at me from his perch on my cubicle wall.

"What? What did you say?"

"I'm sorry, sir." I cover smoothly, because at least the silver lining of acting is that you can course correct on the fly. "I want to make sure this works for *you*. Do you have any other policies you'd like to bundle along with your life insurance policy? We also offer homeowners insurance. It could be available to you for a monthly rate of $106.40."

There's a beat when I brace myself for an unceremonious *click* on the other end of the line. I *really* have to focus. But it's hard, because the evenings are stuffed full of rehearsals. I've even got them jammed into my lunch break. Fittings. Solo rehearsals with a voice coach. I love it, but it's added a level of *swirling storm* to my life that I didn't anticipate.

Kind of like Wes.

"Sure," says the man on the other end of the line, and my thoughts have wandered so far to Wes's body, to the heated look in his eyes when we kiss—when we do *more* than kiss —that, for a split second, I don't know what he's talking about.

"Wonderful. That's wonderful." I sell him on an auto policy too.

Disaster averted.

But it leaves me shaken, somehow off-balance in a way I don't like.

I know what the cure to that is.

Today my lunch break is only a lunch break. No plans, no fittings, no rehearsals. May has turned over into June and I step out into the sunlight, my phone already warm in my hand. It's five minutes after twelve when I dial Summer's number.

She picks up on the first ring. "Oh, my God, it's you! I *miss* you!"

Her words are muffled behind food, but the happiness is unmistakable.

"What's for lunch?"

"A pita from the place down the street." She laughs. "I'm outside on a park bench. What are you eating?"

"I'm going to that gyro cart on the corner by my office. Twins!"

"See? I knew we'd still be linked at the mind even when I moved out."

"Then you should guess what I'm going to say next."

"Let me think." Summer graces me with the sound of her chewing and swallowing another bite of pita. "You're going to somehow shake up my life as I know it."

I was going to say we should make lunch plans for next week, but the moment the words are out of my mouth, all the pieces fall into places. I've been wanting to have Summer and

Dayton over for dinners. I've been wanting to make this thing with me and Wes *real*. I want to burst that bubble between the dreamy beginnings of a relationship, when it's still a secret that nobody knows, and light it up with the world's best spotlight. I'm tired of hiding us in the dark, damn it.

"Of course I am. Find a babysitter, because you're coming to dinner."

"What?" Summer says around another mouthful of pita, and my stomach growls at the frankly disgusting sound. I can't help it. I'm starving. "Tonight?"

"Yes. It's past time that you visited the old stomping grounds, and we need to reconnect on a spiritual level."

I love to hear her laugh. "A *spiritual* level? Does that mean I need to bring dessert?"

"You know that's what it means. You must bring the best dessert you can rustle up on short notice."

"I don't know," she frets. "It *is* short notice. What if I can't find—"

"You will find a sitter. I can sense it," I intone, and Summer laughs again. "This is the spontaneity of life. This is what we have to do in order to keep things fresh and fun. If we don't have unexpected dinners every now and again, what's the point of living?"

There's an ache at the center of my chest that I can't name, but the excitement of making plans with Summer soothes it, lets it fall back to the depths where it belongs.

"What's the point?" she cries. "Get your lunch. I've got to

connect with my babysitter. Do you have any other breaking news?"

The urge to tell her right now, to get it out into the open, is so strong it feels like vertigo. I open my mouth. "No. Nothing at all. See you tonight at seven. Love you."

"Love youuuuu." She disconnects the call in the middle of her profession of affection and I pick up the pace a second time. I could call Wes and let him know...but no. I slip my phone into my purse. It'll be a nice surprise.

I SWEEP into the apartment on an early summer breeze, my arms laden with bags, and sing Wes's name. He appears from the kitchen, wiping his mouth.

"What's all that?"

"Dinner. We're having a little party."

I wait for the corner of his mouth to turn up in the little smile that says, *Whitney, I think you're amazing, and now you have made me see that life is about the last-minute plans we make to ensure a bit of spontaneity in our lives.*

"I already ate."

It sends a frisson of cold through my heart, but I ignore it, brushing past him into the kitchen and letting the bags land heavily on the counter. "No big. It's not until seven, and you're going to *love* who's coming."

"Who did you invite?" Wes stands in the doorway, not breaching the line between the hall and the kitchen, and stuffs his hands into his pockets.

"My best friend in the world, Summer Sullivan. And *your* best friend in the world, Dayton Nash."

"Okay," he says flatly, and I want to die a little. "That could be a little awkward. Pretending we're not—you know. Giving this a try."

"Why would we do that?" I keep myself moving, keep putting things into the fridge. I have a recipe for a chicken pot pie bake that everyone's going to love. It's just the kind of thing to sit at the center of a bunch of laughing, happy friends. Only Wes's eyes are wary and cold. "You don't think we should tell them?"

"I think we should take five seconds and plan it out *together* before we jump in with both feet."

He's pissed.

I feel myself stiffen, feel myself get ready to shoot his anger right back at him, but I look at his shoulders, tensed beneath his shirt, and I don't. I do the opposite.

I go to him. I take his hands. I press his knuckles to my lips.

And then I lick the ridge of his middle finger.

He jerks his hand back with a laugh. "What the fuck, Whit?"

"I should have asked you. I thought it was a nice surprise."

He looks off to the side, his gaze going a little harder. "Don't blindside me with my sister."

I slink closer, pressing my hip against his, forcing myself into the crook of his arm. It takes him a moment, but he relaxes. "Can I blindside you with chicken pot pie bake?" I lower my voice, putting all the sexy vibes I can into my tone.

Honestly, I overshoot it a little. "Can I blindside you with my luscious body?"

"You? Blindside *me*?" He's absolutely still for a moment, and then he sweeps me into his arms, so abruptly I let out a surprised squeak. "No. I'm taking over."

He so, *so* does.

THE WAY WHITNEY REBOUNDS, pouncing on me in the bedroom, already excited and wet, takes the edge off.

A little.

Not enough that the headache goes away, but enough. Enough that I'm not furious with her for springing this on me at the last minute. It's fine. It should be fine. Dayton's my oldest friend, and Summer is her best friend, and there's absolutely no reason we shouldn't have them over for dinner tonight.

I know I hurt Whitney when I didn't get on board with making some strange dating announcement, but Jesus. The tension has curled right up into the base of my neck, and even with her above me, with the delectable curves of her breasts inches from my face, my heart pounds. My mouth is dry. I don't want to fucking do this.

And it has nothing to do with Whitney.

I'm not ashamed of her.

God, how could I be ashamed of her, when I need her this way? When every single inch in my body bends toward her, every single cell, so I can feel the pull of her the moment she enters the room.

"You're so *here*," she whispers, her voice throaty and full of an impending orgasm. "You're so solid."

If this is supposed to be dirty talk, it's the least dirty thing I've ever heard. No—it's not dirty. It's Whitney. She's telling me what she thinks the truth is, the realest, rawest truth, and she's wrong. I'm not fucking solid. I feel like my feet struggle to touch the ground. The only thing keeping me on the bed is the weight of her. The curves of her haul me along to a violent, utilitarian orgasm, hers on top of mine, that makes her laugh.

She jumps off the bed and stretches in a luxurious circle. "Shower with me. I want to wash your hair."

The world rocks underneath me. There are too many avenues to go down when it comes to Whitney washing my hair. My skin vibrates with all the possibilities. It makes my head ache to think about it, which is insane. It's certifiable. Whitney, naked in the shower, servicing *me*? There should be no question.

I wrap her up in my arms and propel her into the bathroom, my muscles settling, now that I'm the one driving the motion. "No time," I say into the crook of her neck. "Not if there are guests coming."

～

WHITNEY THROWS open the door to the apartment two hours

later and screams with unadulterated joy, Summer's answering shriek just as shrill. Dayton reaches for my hand over their shoulders. "You'd think they'd been apart for years." He's barely able to make himself heard over the big reunion.

Summer releases Whitney and follows her into the apartment. "Oh, my God, it's so *different* in here."

"I've kept it mostly the same," says Whit, leading her into the living room like she's a realtor at an open house. "I liked it so much the way it was before."

"It's the vibe," my sister says solemnly. "Much more manly. Much more—" She snaps her mouth shut, her eyes going from me to Whitney and back again. "There's a different vibe."

"Is it the heavenly scent of my cooking?" Whitney bats her eyelashes at her best friend. "Because I'll tell you what. My vibe is hungry." She's beaming, so happy, and I'm surprised she doesn't come right out and say it now. The horrible dread of waiting settles in the pit of my gut. It shouldn't be like this. It should be exciting.

Whitney waits until we're seated around the kitchen table, each person with a face stuffed full of a chicken pot pie casserole that Dayton raves about. Each bite I take is a crapshoot. One moment it's delicious, amazing, the best thing I've ever tasted. Then the next bite is tasteless. Cardboard.

"I have some news," Whitney announces into the quiet, and I see her enjoying the little hop Summer does in her seat, the way her fork clatters to the plate.

"Tell us right now."

"What kind of news, Whit?" My chest seizes. Dayton's totally relaxed. He takes another bite of the food, watching his wife with a certain amusement, his eyes flicking to Whitney across the table. How can he be so calm? How can he be so calm when she's so unpredictable? Doesn't he feel that in the air?

I can't breathe.

Whitney straightens her back, her chin lifting with pride. "I got a part in an off-Broadway show."

"What?" Summer leaps from her seat. "What? Oh, my God, *what*?"

Another crescendo of screams. We're going to get a noise complaint.

"When is it? We have to buy tickets!" Summer is alight with excitement for her friend, and my heart squeezes at the sight of her. She doesn't have a jealous bone in her body, except when it comes to Day. She was always fierce about him. I just didn't want to see it. "Are they selling tickets yet?"

"No." Whitney laughs. "And you don't think I'll set some aside for you? Yeah, right. I need *somebody* in the front row." There's a break in the moment, a crack in Whitney's joy, and it's clear as the morning sun. Summer doesn't seem to notice or feel it. "You have to come. I'll get you the finest babysitter in the city—"

Summer waves her off. "We'll take care of all that. I can't wait. I can't *wait*. When is opening night?"

"Three weeks."

"That soon? Let me put it in my phone. What's the name of

it?" Summer races for her purse, pulls out her phone, and taps the date into it.

"All The Way Home."

"Damn, that sounds *good*. Friday night, right? Day and I will *be* there. Are you coming, Wes?" She looks at me out of the corner of her eye. "You have to, Wes. You've got to bring someone. It would be so fun. A double date."

Whitney's face changes. The moment is being handed to her on a silver platter, and I can't let her have it. I can't. How the hell is she going to paint this? I was never supposed to want her, never supposed to give into the temptation of a whirlwind of a person—

"Whit and I are together." My gruff words fall like a rock onto glass.

Dayton swings his head around toward me, eyebrows raised. Whitney's mouth drops open. Summer doesn't look up from her phone. She's still typing something, her eyebrows knitted together in concentration.

"Whit who? Is that who you're bringing on your date? That's so funny, someone with the same name as—"

"Me," Whitney cuts in. "It's me. Wes and I are together." She clasps her hands in front of her, a compromise between a clasp and a beg, and waits.

"Hold on. What?" Summer pops her head up and looks her friend in the eyes. "Have I crossed over into an alternate universe? You and Wes? *That* Wes?" She cocks her head in my direction without looking at me. "Together? My brother, and you. Together?"

"Yes." Whitney's gone pale, and I realize for the first time that her excitement has masked a fear she had. She was worried about Summer too, even as she pushed and pushed to share the big news.

Summer stares at her, dazed. "Whitney." Her words are slow and deliberate. "Are you fucking with me right now? Because if you are—"

"I'm not. I'm absolutely not, Sunny. Not even a little bit."

"Oh. My. *God*!" Summer shouts the last word and flings herself at Whitney, then to me, grabbing both our hands like we've won some Publishers' Clearing House prize. "You guys! That is—that's *crazy*! Wes, I—" She laughs out loud and Dayton comes over to clap me on the back. "I don't know who I'm more pissed at. My brother or my best friend. You should have *told* me."

"There are certain things in life that require ceremony and planning, and one of those things is telling your best friend that you are dating her older brother, which under any circumstance is fraught with—"

Summer slaps her playfully on the arm. "It's crazy," she says softly, and she keeps saying it again and again, the rest of the night. "It's so crazy. I can't believe it. It's so crazy."

ALL THE WAY HOME, Broadway debut from Rowan Holland, pulls me right into its current, filling my veins with excitement and joy and, oh, God, exhaustion. It's tiring as fuck. That's the only way I can describe it.

I'm not enough of an idiot to quit my job at the insurance agency, but I do use my new womanly confidence and power to sweet-talk my manager into letting me cut my schedule by three hours in the afternoon. Leaving at two is the only thing that saves my sanity. The closer we get to opening night, the farther rehearsals bleed into the afternoon—and into the night.

Ten days before showtime, I get to the theater at 2:45, and I'm sucked directly into the whirlpool frenzy. There must have been some plan going into the show—it can't all be decided at the last moment like this—but you wouldn't know that based on the frenetic pace at which I'm tugged from stage to dressing room and back again.

It's happening right now.

Wanda, a seamstress from the costume department, who has the most glorious blonde curls I've ever seen in my life, is in a very intimate position with my boobs and the top that I wear in the second scene when Mark, the assistant director, hustles in from the hall connecting the theater's basement to the backstage area.

"How's it going, Wanda?"

"Making adjustments." Wanda doesn't take her eyes off the front of my shirt. "It'll be another five."

"Make it two. We need Whit onstage."

I cock my head to the side and keep my torso perfectly still so as not to disturb Wanda's adjustment magic. I didn't see what was wrong with the top when she fussed over it originally, but she's been in the business for fifteen years, and I'm not the type to argue with a true professional.

"Onstage?" I pitch the question as neutrally as possible. It's been four—no, five—hours since I got here straight from work, and it was an intense rehearsal. "We wrapped, didn't we?"

"Oh, yeah. Yeah, that last run was great, but Rowan wants to run a couple scenes one more time. Get it super tight before we dive in to the more extended runs tomorrow afternoon. A couple of notes—"

His notes tumble into one side of my brain and melt away under the stage lights. It's the breakup scene Rowan wants to run, and I'm jittery with all the emotion, at all the blank seats in the front row. I normally don't look at them, but tonight they're drawing my attention like a laser beam is behind my eyes, tracking for that red velvet. And how empty it is. Empty, empty, empty.

I texted Wes two hours ago, saying I'd be home soon. Jesus, was that off.

When I get home, I'm going to jump him. I'm going to give him hurricane-force sex and jolt him right out of his worry. Because he *will* worry. Three times now, he's taken the train and met me at the theater, so I don't have to come home alone. He sits on the aisle in the train, bracing himself against whatever horrors the New York City subway might be saving for me. The man deserves a hot night, and I'm going to give it to him. And despite everything, despite Jason's twisted face, three feet from mine, the heat from the lights and the raised voices curling around us, I smile.

"What was that?" Rowan's voice cuts in, analytical and amazed at the same time. "That was the craziest choice I've ever seen you make."

"I—" Honestly, she hasn't seen me make many choices.

Rowan takes the side stairs two at a time. She plants herself right on the edge and stares me down. Jason, who's been roped into this through no fault of his own, watches with detached interest. He knows as well as I do that Rowan will want to work through this *now* if there's hope of adding more sharp intensity to the scene.

"Let's see that again." She crosses her arms over her chest. She's going to watch this up-close, which means micro-managing every moment. It can be frustrating as hell, this method, but when she's finished, we have these shining jewels of moments that don't feel hard to access at all.

But then—Wes.

I open my mouth to ask for one minute—one text—but Rowan claps her hands. "From the top."

Guilt swoops down the back of my neck and settles in my gut, but it's burned away in a flare of tired excitement. Usually, I'm the one driving these last-minute attacks on expectations and routine, but Rowan's white-knuckling the driver's seat, and all I can do is come along for the ride.

I'm sure Wes will understand.

I THROW OPEN the side door of the theater, trying to take my phone out at the same time, and run headlong into a chest that's as hard as a brick wall. He's moving so fast it knocks the wind out of me.

"Shit. Fuck—" I reel backward, into the doorframe, and he catches me with sure hands. Wes. "Jesus, Wes, I thought you were a mugger."

"You don't want to know what I thought." His hands move over my arms, my waist, light touches everywhere, as if he's confirming that I'm real and alive.

I push into him, letting his arms fall heavily around me, and squeezing tight. "Rehearsal ran late."

"I can fucking see that now."

I take his hand and pull back, so I can look him in the eyes. "God, you're sweet."

"I'm not trying to be—"

"Let's go to dinner."

Wes's eyes flash. "What?"

"Let's go to dinner. I'm starving. And it's a beautiful night." I tip my head back and look up toward the sky. There's too much light pollution to see the stars, but it's an inky orange above Manhattan and I want to be out in it. I want to be eating and drinking and forgetting. I want to fill the last remaining void with food and laughter. "Let's wake up Summer and Day and go out. Wasn't that so much fun?"

He stares down at me, face impassive, and then he squeezes my hand. It feels like pity. "Come on, Whit. Let's go home."

"Are we really that boring?" I draw a fingertip down the front of his shirt—gray and plain and somehow one of the sexiest things I've ever seen on a man. "I want to go *out*. This day has been never-ending, and I'm so hungry, and—"

"There's food at the apartment." He pulls away, toward the street. I can feel him, pulling toward home, and I don't want to go that way. All of my energy sparks in the opposite direction. I'm not sure where, exactly, that *is,* but those are just details. We can figure the rest out on the fly.

"But it's not *exciting.*" The city is still awake around us. Taxis whip by on 45th, and someone's bachelorette party whoops by on the sidewalk. I want to be *in* that. I need to be in that. I need to be far away from here, from the exhaustion settling in over my shoulders like a too-heavy coat, from that barren first row of seats. I know that sounds crazy. Of course nobody's going to be sitting in the first row during rehearsal, but the sight of it— "We've got the whole city, right here at our feet, Wes, and—"

The pressure disappears from my hand and Wes moves in close, so close that the air is full of him, that my skin is full of him. Hands on my face. Tension sings through his palms. They're rough. Not desk-job hands. It sends a shiver racing over the curves of my shoulders. "I don't give a fuck about the city. Do you understand?" I'm melting in his grip, even while a part of me—a part of me deep down inside that I can't squeeze into submission—struggles against the ringing authority in his voice. "Do you get that, Whit? Why would I care about the city when I've got the entire world in my hands?"

Me. He means me.

It's the rawest admission, straight from the center of his soul, and my next breath sears into my lungs. "Wes—"

"Don't argue with me." Determination flares in his green eyes, reflected in the glow from the streetlight at the end of the alley. "You can't keep doing this. You can't keep waltzing off into God knows where—"

"We both know where. We're both standing in the same city. If you'd only come with me, you'd see that—"

He presses closer and it's so intimate that I half want to give in. We're both wearing a surplus of clothes, and I want all of Wes's body in light like this, murky and golden and glorious.

I also want the loud crush of a bar, the din of people shouting over one another, that heady, drunk feeling where nothing is wrong and everything has always been right.

"Do you ever *listen*?" Wes growls the words, his eyes searching mine. "Do you ever shut up for two seconds and listen?"

"No. I never do. I thought that was what you liked about me."

"Jesus, Whit, you're so—" He looks down into my face. "You're so fucking frustrating. You don't even know what you're walking into. I came here to make sure—"

To make sure I was safe. That's what he's about to say, and suddenly I can't bear to hear it. I'm a grown woman. I can handle this situation. "I'm *fine*, Wes, I'm really fine." I shift my weight back, pulling away, and he won't have it. The excitement in my gut curdles to a fine, hot irritation. "I was going to get the subway and come home. Christ, you don't have to be such a control freak."

He drops his hands away from my face and the summer air feels cold against my skin. "Are you fucking kidding me?"

"You're going to have to get over it, one of these days."

His expression goes hard. "Get over what, exactly?"

"The difficult schedule." I run a hand over my hair. It's a mess. I've had clothes tugged on and off all night, and not in the fun way. "I get that it's hard for you to get out of your routine, but—"

He backs up another step. "I'm not out of any *routine*. You haven't been around for the last few weeks, so maybe you haven't noticed, but that *routine* is the reason you always have food to eat when you come home at one in the morning—"

"I can't *help* that. They scheduled evening rehearsals to accommodate me, so—"

"That's not the *point*, Whit. The point is, I've built a life to keep us both afloat, and you're here trying to convince me that heading out into the city in the middle of the fucking night is the responsible thing to do—"

"I'm trying to convince you that *responsibility* isn't the only way to live on the earth, for God's sake, and if you never stop being so rigid and fucking boring—"

"I'd rather be rigid and boring than an erratic idiot who doesn't care about anyone else."

"You know what? You know *what*?" The hurt hits while I'm still spitting the words, a shockwave like a secondary earthquake, the ground lurching beneath my feet. "If I'm so *erratic* and *stupid*—"

"You *are*!" Wes explodes. I can see him vibrating with the effort to maintain some sort of stillness. "Fuck. You're not stupid. You know I didn't mean that. But you spend half your time dragging us off into bullshit that I—"

"Into bullshit that you'd *never* try on your own because you're too obsessed with your precious routine! God, what *happened* to you in the Army, Wes?" I can't wipe the sneer from my face. It's ugly. I can feel it. I just can't stop it, stop the bubbling hurt—

"I hope you never find out," he thunders. "That's why I'm here, in the middle of the fucking night, because I don't want you to find out what it's like."

"I'm not in a war zone. What's *wrong* with you?"

He shakes his head. "You're blind. You're just blind to it. You think this is a fucking game. You think this is all a fun little game, and you don't care what happens."

His words settle in, a dark haze, and I feel every single moment of work today, of rehearsal, of the emotionally draining work on the stage, those empty seats, everything. "Fuck off, Wes."

He shoves his hands in his pockets and looks over his shoulders, checking once, twice. "That's what you really want? Me to fuck right off and leave you alone? Because fucking Christ, Whitney, I'll do it."

"Yeah." I spit the word at him like a curse. "Yeah, I do."

His jaw works, and the next instant, his hand is locked on my elbow, pulling me toward the street. It's like I weigh nothing. Like I'm not dragging my heels, even though I most definitely am. I pound a fist ineffectually against his hand.

"Hey, asshole, I said *fuck off*, and this isn't—"

He tugs me right along to the curb and one step into the street and oh, my God, am I going to have to scream? Am I going to have to make a huge scene in front of the theater? My colleagues are going to be walking out at any second—

Wes looks into the street and swings his other hand into the air. The traffic rushes into my vision then—two blue cars and a yellow cab behind them both, its light on. The cab swings to the curb in front of us.

"What—"

He wrenches the door open with his free hand and then, with so much gentleness I almost die right then and there, he lowers me into the backseat. His face is a thunderstorm. Wes leans in behind me, almost on top of me, and tosses some folded bills up toward the cabby. He reels off our address—my address. "Get her home safely. I've got your cab number. Do you hear me?"

"I've got it," says the cab driver, and then Wes slams the door behind me.

I can't breathe.

I twist in my seat, looking for him. I want to finish this conversation. It doesn't feel finished. It feels like a nightmare. But all I see the line of his shoulders, disappearing from a pool of light into a pool of darkness down the block. He's already gone. He's done what I asked and fucked right off.

"You all right?" The cabbie's eyes meet mine in the rearview mirror. I'm crying. I raise a hand to wipe the tears from my cheeks. I'm going to need a towel. "I don't have to take you where he said. I can take you anywhere."

I swallow a jagged sob and straighten my back. "No, he was right." The words taste bitter, acrid. "He was right."

"—IF YOU WERE DOING OKAY."

I catch the tail end of the sentence, like it's coming at me underwater, the sound waves distorted and strange. My head breaks the surface and instead of clean, fresh air, instead of the deep, cleansing breaths of childhood summers in Michigan, it's the recycled air of my cubicle at Visionary Response. Greg hovers near the door. He's watching me, and I've been—

I don't know what I've been doing.

When I sat down forty-five minutes ago, I had every intention of preparing a summary of the rebuild of the client project in the suburbs. I was right about it—it wasn't stripping out one thing and substituting another, it was a complete rebuild.

I had it under control until I walked away from Whitney a week ago.

A long, agonizing week ago.

Greg is expecting an answer.

"Yep. Yeah." I turn around in my chair, hoping to look casual and probably fucking failing. "Everything's good. I'm working on a summary now. On your desk this afternoon."

He considers me. "I hope you know that all these changes are client-side, Wes. It seems like it's weighing on you, and I don't want you to get the wrong idea."

"No, no. I got it. It's good. It's—" I'm about to say *something to focus on* but that would be a stupid thing to tell my boss, that I need something to focus on. I let myself sink into this project like a drowning man because Whitney is like the sun. Even though she's not *mine* anymore, I can't ignore her. She shines through the windows in the morning and sets in my heart at night. It's fucking terrible. "It's good to see things from another perspective." It sounds lame and untrue and feels that way on my tongue.

Greg just nods. "You were in early this morning."

"Yeah. I'll have this to you any time—"

"Did you eat breakfast?"

I blink at him. "Uh, no."

"It's almost twelve-thirty. Get some lunch. Come back fresh."

I want to ask him what it is, exactly, that's making him think I'm not up to the job. I hadn't planned on lunch out—I planned on working straight through and leaving early. And I know, I *know*, that if I push hard enough, he'll leave me alone.

But he's my boss, and I'm fucking tired. I'm tired of everything. I'm tired of the cheap hotel I'm staying at, two blocks away. I'm tired of missing Whitney.

I'm tired of fighting.

The last thing on earth I want to do is eat lunch with Greg, so I stand up as if he's released me from a sentence involving putting together this summary, and pat my pocket for my wallet. "You, uh—"

He raises both hands. "I already ate. You go on."

Outside on the sidewalk, with the afternoon sun beating down on my face, I can't stand it.

It's so fucking abrasive, the way Whitney always yanks me out of my plans, the way she's always trying to stir things up, to make life unpredictable. It's abrasive and dangerous. But right now, I wish she'd appear on the corner and drag me to some ridiculous, shady hole-in-the-wall and talk my ears off about the mayhem that is an Off-Broadway show. I don't know how those people ever get anything done, and deep down, I don't care, but if I could just see her lips move around those words—bright lipstick, dark hair, eyes dancing—she could talk about anything.

God, I'm so fucking pathetic.

There's only one other person who knows how pathetic I feel.

I pull my phone out of my pocket.

"Wes?"

I haven't even dialed Dayton's number.

I blink into the sun.

It's not Dayton.

It's fucking Ben Powell.

"Is there anywhere on earth you won't follow me, you fucking stalker?"

He cracks a smile and hitches that damn backpack up on his shoulder. "You're right about one thing. I was looking for you."

"We have nothing to talk about, man." The bristles rise on the back of my neck.

"That's not what it looks like. You look like you just got kicked to the curb. Are you fired?"

"What are you *doing* here?"

"I told you. Looking for you."

"I never told you where I work."

"Well, you signed up for fucking LinkedIn. Don't act like we're in the nineteenth century, bro."

Jesus, he's annoying.

"So, is it still current? You look pretty forlorn out here."

I rub at that knot in the back of my neck. "I didn't get *fired*."

"Then she left."

I stare at him. "How the hell are you so sure of yourself? You disappear for months, and now you want to be my fucking therapist?"

He laughs, like everything in the world is fine. "I do *not* want to be your therapist. I wanted to give you something."

"Let's not. Let's not do a gift exchange outside my office."

"That would be a shitty exchange, because I'm sure you don't have anything for me. Look." He reaches around and unzips his backpack. I fight the urge to sprint in the other direction. I can't see what's in the damn backpack and every nerve screams a warning. I'm on edge like I've never been on edge, and it's Powell—I should be able to trust him with my life. I don't even trust the breeze.

"Powell—"

"Shut it, Sullivan, and look."

He withdraws his hand.

There, resting against his palm, is a jagged piece of metal. It's twisted and torn, maybe four inches long. The sight of it turns the heat of the summer breeze into a desert wind and the hum of distant traffic into the treads of our Humvee against that gravel.

"What the fuck is that?"

"It's the answer." There's wonder in Powell's voice. He sounds like Afghanistan was a grand adventure, some kind of epic fucking fairy tale, where we were honorable knights and all of us came home in one piece, with nothing but a few scratches in the armor.

"The answer to what?" Blood thrums in my ears, competing with the sound of the traffic, and a bead of sweat drips down my back underneath my shirt. I've got to get off the sidewalk.

"To why." He lets his hand hover in the air for a few more

moments, then closes his fist around the strip of metal. The instant it's out of sight, my lungs release and I take a deep breath, my vision clearing.

"I don't believe it." I take one step to the side. I'm going to shove past the bastard, call Dayton from the corner, and tell him to meet me at the bar. I need a fucking drink. Or several.

Powell's hand is a solid stop sign in the center of my chest. "You haven't let me convince you."

"I don't need convincing. I'm not going to believe it."

He moves back in front of me, and I hate with a violent fury how level his gaze his, how self-confident he is. "Why'd your girl leave you, Sullivan?"

I clench my teeth.

We face off on the sidewalk.

"You're a piece of shit."

Powell claps me on the shoulder. "You pick the place. I'll buy the first round."

MACMILLAN'S IS the easiest place to go. Where the hell else am I going to pick? I'm fuming and trying to hide it.

"Yeah." Powell leans back in the booth like he's been here a thousand times. "You do need a beer."

"No shit." I rub both hands over my face and snatch up the list of beers on tap. They all blur together. Powell doesn't give me the chance to agonize over it. He orders two Sam

Adams from the waitress who buzzes by, her ponytail bouncing in the afternoon sunlight coming through the front window, then thinks better of himself. He catches her on the way to the bar and stabs a thumb back over his shoulder at me. She blushes. She blushes *red*. I throw the drink menu back onto the table and press my palms into the cool surface.

He comes back to the booth and slides in, looking every bit as relaxed as when we first came in. Nothing bothers this guy. I hate him. And then—I don't. We spent a lot of hours together on two separate deployments, and there's something steadying about his attitude. I wouldn't call him easygoing, exactly, but not a lot rattles him. It's also infuriating. I'm fucking rattled, and it's been rolling to a boil since last week.

"You want to talk about it?"

I glare at him.

"Not until the beers come," he says. "Got it."

"Not ever."

He spreads both hands open in front of him. "Low risk, buddy. Why'd she leave? I'm assuming she left, by how sad puppy you looked out in front of that office."

"You *really* didn't have to come here. I'm not looking for any answers."

Powell smiles and it looks easy. "That's the thing about answers. Sometimes they find you."

"Stop being a cryptic asshole."

"Fine. I'll go first." He looks out the front window of the bar

—arranging his thoughts? I don't know—and turns back to me. "I'm sorry for heading off the grid there for a while, man. That was a shitty thing to do."

"I'm all grown up, Powell. You don't have to chase me to New York City every time you get a guilty conscience."

"I left to find out more about that incident."

"I—"

He lifts one hand and I bite back the rest of the words on the tip of my tongue. "It didn't seem right, you know? We spent weeks waiting around for final orders. Even Day was in on the planning. He'd have never driven us right into a known IED."

"Lots of IEDs are unknown. That's the fucking point of them."

"But this one shouldn't have been." Powell's eyes focus on a spot in the distance, then come back to meet mine. "It shouldn't have been. You remember that outpost."

I'll never fucking forget that little village, tucked up next to the mountains like a kid tucked under his mother's arm. They'd been completely fucked over by an insurgent group there, and the people were in an impossible situation. Get too buddy-buddy with the Americans, and the insurgents would make them pay for it. Trade help for their lives, and they'd pay for it. We were going to flush out the last of the insurgents. They were supposed to be the last.

"Get to the point." I taste the grit in my mouth and wish the beers would hurry up and get here.

"They were focused on minimizing casualties. That's what made the whole thing ring false to me."

"What does it matter, Powell?" My head throbs. "What the fuck does it matter if it rang *false?* It happened." It happened, and I can still hear Dayton screaming, right now.

The waitress *thunks* down a beer in front of me and I grab it like a life preserver. One swig doesn't clear the grit from my teeth, but the second one does.

Powell watches me, waiting, maddeningly patient. "Doesn't it feel like a ring around your neck?"

As if in answer, the knot at the base of my skull throbs. "What about it? It was four seconds in the course of four deployments—"

"There's nobody else here, Sullivan. Cut the bullshit."

I don't want to admit it to him, but I'm a husk of a man. My skin offers no protection from the elements. My heart aches. "Fine. It does."

"You were driving. Your best friend planned the mission. It could have gone worse. God knows that. I've lain awake enough nights because of how close it came." He looks into his beer. "The heat of it."

I can feel it scorching my skin, even now. "I know all of this, Powell. The point. The *point.*"

"I had to know what was at the heart of it." He breathes in through his nose and I swear to God, everyone in Macmillan's is looking at us. "There's some stuff that's random, and some that's avoidable. I wanted to know which one it was."

"Are you always this fucking irritating?" I take another drink of my beer. "Seriously, Powell, I'd rather eat alone if you're going to string me along like this."

"It wasn't avoidable, but it also wasn't random."

I stare him down. The man digs into his backpack again, pulling out the shrapnel. My throat closes.

"It was a different group of insurgents. You've heard about them on TV, yeah?"

I don't watch the news much anymore, but this is a semantic difference, so I nod. Of course I've seen about the new groups rising in the Middle East. We couldn't even stamp out the one we went there for. It's like a hydra. Unlimited heads.

"This was a new one of theirs. Slimmer tech, and they planted it after the scouts came and went."

I close my eyes and search the memory. "Couldn't have. There were no marks. Not that I—"

"There were no marks because it was smaller than the other shit. It was thinner. They didn't dig up the ground to bury it —they cut a layer off the top of the earth and put it right back down where it was. You didn't miss it, man. And neither did Day, or the guys on the team that assessed the area. You were driving blind."

I can't speak, so I drink my beer instead.

Powell drops the shrapnel back into his bag and closes it with a practiced finality. "That's what I came here to tell you. I wanted to show it to you before we parted ways."

I clear my throat. It's fucking difficult. "How'd you—" Powell raises his eyebrows, a little gleeful. "You're not supposed to have that. That's—"

"I spent some time asking questions. I spent some time looking. Effort. Results. All that."

"Can I see it again?"

He doesn't hesitate. He opens his bag, pulls it out, and drops it into my palm.

It's surprisingly light, for a piece of the thing that almost killed me.

All this time, I thought I was the one who pulled it out of the earth, who set the thing in motion that took Dayton's leg and my sanity, and Powell's ability to stay grounded in a fucking city like an adult. It was the same, in my mind, as putting it there in the first place.

"You had nothing to do with that," Powell says, and leans back to let the waitress deliver our burgers.

I hand it back to him in silence.

"You can hold the wheel as tight as you want." He adds ketchup and stacks on the pickles from the bed of lettuce and tomatoes on the side of his plate. "Sometimes, you still get blown up."

"ARENʼT YOU, like, three days out from opening night? I thought you'd be booked solid."

Summer glows in the seat across from me at Vino, wearing her favorite summer halter top. She looks damn good, even though I can tell she did her makeup in a hurry. In her defense, I only called her forty minutes ago and begged pathetically for a girls' night out. Or a girls' two hours out. Whatever she could spare.

The wine is delicious, sweet and sparkling, and I try to throw myself into it without success. "I kicked ass at rehearsal today. Bargained for an early morning tomorrow instead of a late night tonight. How's January and Day?"

"Oh, she's been asleep since eight and he's tucked on the couch with a beer, so I'd say they're living their best life. What about you? Did you miss me? That chicken pot pie bake was amazing, by the way."

"Yes. I only wish my life was as successful as the chicken pot pie bake."

Summer raises her eyebrow. "I'd say you're being dramatic, but you're always a little dramatic, and this actually seems...serious."

God, this is mortifying. I twist the stem of my wine glass in my fingers. Should I *really* have asked Summer here? She's Wes's sister. This is exactly why I never should have touched him in the first place.

She might be Wes's sister, but she's my best friend, so screw it.

"The show is going really, really well. Rowan thinks there's enough buzz about opening night that we might get a few new investors in attendance. Maybe a Broadway run in the spring."

"That's so exciting, Whit." Summer beams at me, but the smile slips off her face as quickly as it rose. "But you look like you found a bug in your wine glass."

"Yes, well—" I can't bring myself to say *he dumped me* or even *I dumped him* because what really did happen? A stupid fight? There was no misunderstanding, that's for sure. We both said things we meant. I only wish now that I hadn't said them. Some of them anyway. "My personal life has become a barren, soulless wasteland."

Summer blinks at me. Processing. Processing. Then it hits. "Oh, my God. You and Wes?"

I nod mournfully, which fucking sucks, because we're at Vino and there should be no mourning in this place, unless you really like mourning in wine bars. Not between me and Summer, is what I mean.

I stare down into my wine glass, wishing there really was a

bug in there so I'd have a reason to watch the bubbles rise from the bottom like an idiot. An *erratic* idiot, if Wes is correct, which, maybe he is. I don't know. What I *do* know is that I don't want to look at Summer. Perfect, honorable Summer. I can't bear the disappointment in her eyes.

"Whit, I'm so sorry." Her tone makes me raise my eyes from the bottom of my glass. There's no hint of disapproval. It's pure sympathy. "Listen, I—" She purses her lips, making her mind up about something. "I don't blame you. At all."

"You don't? It would be reasonable to blame me, you know. Wes does. He blames it on—" I roll my eyes toward the ceiling to keep the tears from spilling out. "I don't want to relive the whole thing, but he took issue with some of the more...eccentric aspects of my personality."

Summer's mouth curves in a smile. "Like the way you always like to change plans at the last minute?"

"You could say that."

"Yeah." She shakes her head, her expression settling into a contemplative set. "Day mentioned something like that to me."

"That bastard. He was complaining about me behind my back?"

"No, no, no. *Dayton* mentioned it on his own. That Wes has had...you know, some issues since he got out of the Army. Even before, I guess. Since...the thing with the Humvee."

"Issues that would make him behave like a controlling asshole?"

"Not that it's an excuse—I'm *not* saying that it's an excuse—but yeah. That kind of thing." Summer sighs. "Day's worried about him. He keeps trying to—" She closes her fists around the air. "If he can keep everything under control, nothing like that might happen again. I guess it...boiled over."

"Good for him." It comes out tinged with acid. "He's getting exactly what he wants. A life he can control completely. It's too bad I wasn't like that."

"No, it's not. You're exactly the person you're supposed to be." Summer sips her wine. "Honestly, I loved you guys together."

I exhale hard. I'm *not* crying. Not now. Not at Vino. Not with Summer. "Honestly, I did too. That habit he had of making dinner at the same time every day? I don't know if that was him or whatever this fucked-up nonsense is—"

Summer waves a hand in the air. "Oh, he was always organized. The Army brought out more of that in him. And then...maybe too much."

The center of my chest is a black hole, all the pain of the world sucked into the center. I sniff. "That's no way to live."

"Sometimes people take it to the opposite extreme."

"Summer Sullivan." I put a hand to my chest and throw my widest, most appalled eyes at her. "Are you taking his *side* in this catastrophe of lost love?"

"I'd never take someone's side over yours." She takes another delicate, measured sip of her wine and rolls it around her tongue for a moment before she swallows. "All I'm saying is—"

"Don't."

"All right."

She falls silent, watching the comings and goings of Vino as they swirl around our table.

"I hate when you do that."

"Do what?" Summer is the picture of innocence.

"Listen to me when I'm wrong."

She takes a calm, cleansing breath. "You sounded pretty agonized when you called. And not just normal stress, either. Not just show stress. Not audition stress."

"I never should have agreed to live with you."

"First"—Summer grins—"you asked *me* to live with you, at the beginning of all this. And second, you know you were a wreck, and that's why you called me here. And I came. That should count for something."

"It does."

"You can overcome this, if your heart is broken the wrong way."

It's something Summer's said to me before—a broken heart the wrong way. There are some broken hearts you have to suffer through, because it's ultimately the right thing, or something you have to accept.

I have the horrible, sinking feeling that this is both.

"I don't know, Sunny. It all feels wrong. Everything."

"Give it a few days," she says, too wise for the blonde-haired small-town girl she used to be. "Do your show. Then decide. There's always time to fix things."

I nod with her, and we solemnly "cheers" our wine glasses. Then we move on to other things.

But the truth beats hard in my chest: there's not always time. I can hear it, even now, ticking away.

30

WES

DAYTON OPENS the door after a single knock, wearing boxers and a t-shirt. He doesn't have his leg on. He must have taken the stairs three at a time on one foot to get here before I knocked a second time.

"Hey." He says it as casually as a person can when they're balanced against a doorframe, running a hand through sleep-disheveled hair.

"I woke you up." The guilt balled tightly in the center of my chest is covered in a thick layer of not giving a fuck and giving entirely too many fucks.

"Yeah, and I'm already down here, so don't give me that 'aww shucks' bullshit and walk away." He doesn't ask me what I need. He backs up a step and gestures me inside, then shuts the door gently behind us. "Did you get kicked out of your hotel?"

"How'd you know about the hotel?" It's one in the morning, and I've been fighting off racing thoughts all night. What the hell did I miss?

"Your sister, named Summer." Dayton's voice is gravelly with sleep and the guilt rises again. Not enough to make me leave, but it's there, always there, just like that fucking Humvee. "She has a certain level of friendship with—"

"I never told her I was staying in a hotel."

"Hotel, hostel, somewhere else. You're picky as hell about roommates. Everybody knows that."

"Wes? Are you okay?"

Summer comes down the stairs in bare feet, a soft outfit setting off her hair, which falls loosely around her face.

"You don't have to be up for this."

"The hell I don't." She steps to Day's side and wraps her arm around his waist like it's the easiest thing she's ever done. "You're practically naked."

He looks down at himself. "You're right. I'm not dressed for the occasion. Be right back."

Dayton goes for the stairs and Summer looks at me across the entry hall. "You want a beer?"

"You really don't have to—"

"I'll take that as a yes. And keep your voice down. January did *not* want to go to sleep at bedtime."

I follow Summer into the kitchen. She grabs three beers from the fridge and motions me out onto the back patio. Their backyard isn't huge, but it's got honest-to-God grass, and it's all theirs. I don't know how they lucked into this place.

Sunny sets the beers on a little wicker table and bends over a little firepit in the center of the patio. Her hand works at a switch and it blazes to life, the flames cheerful in the metal sculpted basin.

"Nice, right?" Her face looks oddly proud in the firelight. "I thought it was stupid, but Day wanted it. Turns out he was right."

She goes back to the table and hands me one of the beers. "What's up, Wes? Can't sleep?"

I crack a grin. We used to run into each other in the middle of the night, two teenage ghosts in the hallways of our parents' house. It was easier to talk to her then, in the dark, because there was no front to keep up.

"No. Haven't slept."

Sunny sits in one of the patio chairs and tucks her feet beneath her. It's warm enough not to need a blanket. I've just let my ass hit the wicker when Dayton comes out and takes the third beer, falling into a seat next to Summer.

Now it feels awkward.

I've hauled them out of bed in the middle of the night like a lovesick asshole.

Dayton opens his beer and takes a long drink. "You know," he says thoughtfully, tilting his head back to look at the orange city sky, "if you wanted a night out of that fucking hotel, you could have come here earlier."

I rub my free hand over my face. "I worked late. It...wasn't a problem until later on anyway."

Until later, when the traffic noise was enough to drive a person insane, when someone started a fight in the room below mine, when all I wanted was a breath of Whitney's shampoo and all I could smell was the reek of musty carpet.

"Couch is open. But"—a yawn stretches his face—"maybe I'm an old man now, but I don't have all night to listen to you bitch and moan." Summer gives him a playful slap on the shoulder. "I mean, we're here for you. Tell us all your problems."

I look at them, sitting there in their happiness, with their cold beers and bedhead, and I'm at a loss. What the fuck am I supposed to say? *I want what you have, and I could have had it with Whitney?* It's all so viscerally pathetic that I have to hunt for the words.

I open my mouth.

Dayton tenses, his back coming to attention, and he and Summer both turn their heads toward the house. The backs of my hands tingle with adrenaline. What's going on? What are they *doing*?

The sound hits me a moment later—a thin, high wail.

Day doesn't hesitate. He gets up out of his seat, taking his beer with him, and strides into the house. Summer relaxes back into her seat, her blue eyes flickering along with the fire.

"You could get her back, you know." She raises the beer to her lips and drinks, the movement delicate somehow.

"I will wait for *dawn* if it means having this conversation with Day instead of you."

"I appreciate the vote of confidence, asshole." Summer's

eyes sparkle at her own snappy comeback. "It's an easy choice, Wes. You can either suffer, or you can listen to me."

"It's all suffering."

She rolls her eyes. "Fine. I'm happy to let you dangle on a hook of your own misery until—"

"Just say what you have to say. It's late."

"Says the man who woke me up in the middle of the night."

"You were never supposed to be part of this." In every way possible, she was never supposed to be part of this. *I* was never supposed to be part of this.

"You made a bad mistake with Whitney, but you can fix this. And you should, because she keeps calling me for emergency lunches, and I can see she's been crying underneath her makeup. It's terrible, Wes. She's devastated."

The heat rises in the pit of my gut. "It's never going to work out. She doesn't understand that I'm trying to—"

"Beat the world into submission with your bare hands?"

Summer looks at me steadily over the fire. She radiates an obnoxious calm. There's probably no question in her mind that Day is going to come back and sit right next to her, and here I am, aching for Whitney to be curled up in the next chair over. Her absence is a visceral wound, and I caused it myself.

"You know you can't do that all on your own."

It's not a question.

"I know."

"Wes…"

"I fucking called, okay? This morning. I called the VA. I'll go talk to whatever shrink they want. Okay? I get it. I fucking get it." One phone call doesn't release the pressure in my mind. It can't. And not even tomorrow's emergency appointment will do that. Because the pressure has a shape, and a name. Ben Powell's voice had the ring of truth to it, and it hasn't stopped ringing yet.

Sunny presses her lips together, and her eyes shine brighter in the firelight. "That's—" She nods, her fingertips rising to her lips. "I'm proud of you." She could go farther. She must know that Dayton tried to convince me it would be a good idea to do some talk therapy at the very minimum. But Summer isn't a little girl anymore, needling me to get attention. She's an equal.

"Don't be fucking proud of me. It took losing her to figure it out. The price is a little steep."

She gets up from her chair, leaving the beer on the wicker table, and comes around to me, leaning down to wrap her arms around my neck. Her touch tears at the wound around my heart, scraping and bleeding, and I swallow back a painful lump in my throat.

"You can't stop me. I'm still proud. I know—" She breathes in and I see it then, how close she's been to Dayton's own hurt all this time. How she carries the weight of it on her own shoulders to lessen his burden. "I know."

I see how Whitney, in her own way, tried to do that for me.

And I see the chasm between us, now that I left her. Now that I did her fucking bidding and left her, and wrenched myself away from the one person that made this life seem worth fixing.

Summer straightens up, wiping at her eyes. "Listen to me."

"I've been listening. What do you think—"

She drops into the chair next to me and looks me in the eye. "In all the time you've been with Whitney, haven't you ever stopped to think about *why* she is the way she is? God knows it can be tiring. And...over the top sometimes. But you know why, right?"

I take another swig of beer and pull myself together. "I assume she's always been that way. I've always been on top of my life, and she's always been—I don't know, flighty."

"She is that way because of her dad."

Whitney's face comes back to me then, red-eyed, desolate. "She told me about her dad."

"How much did she tell you?"

"That he was—" The conversation seems like a million years ago. "That he was kind of an asshole, and he was killed by a drunk driver."

"From what she told me, he wasn't a very good dad. He was the kind of man who always wanted to have a good time, and he hated it when Whitney had different ideas about what that meant. They'd fight. But they were alike in ways, you know? When things were good, they were *good*. That last fight—" Summer shakes her head. "It must have been awful for them both."

"It must have been, but I don't see what that has to do with *this*."

"Everything, Wes. Whitney took that to heart. She knows the clock is ticking. On life, I mean. Which sounds morbid and totally depressing, but she knows it can all go away in an instant. And I think, on some level, her dad felt that too."

We're silent for a moment.

"It's obviously a complicated situation, but I think that Whitney is the way she is because she's trying to live up to an idealized version of what he would have been like. She's trying to seize every moment she possibly can. Make it all magical."

She's got that right.

"And then...you know, if one of us were in a Broadway show, Mom and Dad would be in the front row."

"Of course they would be. It would be embarrassing as fuck, with how Mom can get."

"Whit's mom has never been in the picture. And her dad won't be in the front row on Friday. And even if they fought—"

"She'd still want him to be proud of her. Jesus Christ." I drop my head into my hands. "Well, that settles it. I need to pack up and move on. I took that pain and dug into it with my own nails."

"Oh, stop, Wes. Have you talked to her since you two split?"

"No."

"She's a mess. And she misses that you cooked *dinner* at the same time. That's"—her mouth drops open while she searches for the words—"unprecedented. The Whitney I know and love would never allow herself to get excited over something as pedestrian and predictable as dinner at the same time. You were good for her."

"Yes. That's why she wanted me to fuck off."

"Maybe she wanted you to fuck off because she was pissed. And hurting. And maybe she regrets it."

"I'm not waking her up in the middle of the night to find out."

"Ah, the courteous prince. No, don't wake her up in the middle of the night. Don't do *anything* in the middle of the night. It's almost always a bad idea."

"Then what do I do?" It's a pathetic question, and one I would never say out loud in broad daylight. I would never ask my younger sister for this kind of advice. I'm only skating across the edges of complete humiliation because of the hour. And because every inch of me is on fire with pain. With missing her.

"She's never going to stop looking for you, Wes. Show her that she's been found."

"Jesus, Sunny, that's the most cryptic thing you've ever said to me. How the fuck am I supposed to do that?"

"I know exactly how. All you have to do is follow through."

I lean my elbows on my knees and look into the fire. "This is fucked up. I shouldn't even be asking you for help. I shouldn't be asking anyone."

Summer sighs, then reaches over and pats me on the back. "No. You should have asked a long time ago. Get used to it, buddy."

She unfolds herself from the chair and makes her way back toward the house. "Turn the fire off when you're done staring into it. There's an extra blanket in the closet." She's quick, light on her feet, and at the back door in a heartbeat.

"Hey, Sunny?"

"Yeah?" She pauses with her hand on the door, looking back with her expression open, the hint of a smile on her face.

"Thanks."

She blows me a kiss with her fingertips and goes inside.

THE SHOW CAN'T GO on.

I stare at myself in the bright-ass lights of the mirror in my dressing room. The words ring in my ears. The show can't go on. *I* can't go on.

For one thing, I am abjectly unqualified to play the lead role in even an off-Broadway show. Rowan made the biggest mistake of her life when she cast me. Though, in fairness, she couldn't have known that my life would become a complete train wreck a week before opening night.

The world is empty without Wes. I'd take the sight of his shoulders in the streetlight over the nothingness that is my apartment. But what the fuck am I supposed to do? I can't bring myself to text him. I can't bring myself to send that message out into the void, knowing that something inside me has broken us irreparably.

God, it's making me stupidly nostalgic for all those little things about him. The way he'd check the lock on the door before we went to bed for the night, even when he's the one who locked it when we came in. The way he always insisted on walking on the outer edge of the sidewalk, even if we were separated from the street by planters and trees. He was always on the lookout, and being in that sphere of the things he cared about—it was breathtaking. I watch my stupid face contort in the mirror.

There's a knock at the door. "Whit, five minutes to curtain."

"Okay, great!" Can Rowan tell how fucking false I sound right now? Can she tell how miserable I am? I can't bear it. I can't bear to see that empty seat in the front row.

I take a deep, steadying breath. This is what acting *is*. Even though my heart is a wasteland of pain and regret, I will still play the part I've been hired to play. This is my *dream* coming true.

The victory is pretty fucking hollow, I'll tell you that. It's a terrible realization, to find out how much I was counting on Wes. On that strength. Even if that strength was getting the better of him.

"It's for the best," I say, right as my dressing room door swings open.

"What's for the best? Oh, my God, you look so *good*!" Summer is all sleek blonde hair and black date night halter top and joy, and for the smallest moment, I hate her.

Then she throws her arms around me, careful to keep her own face out of my stage makeup, and I love her again. "How'd you get back here?"

"I gave the guy at the door a big smile. And I told him you had to see me before you went onstage." She takes a step back and looks me up and down. "Whitney, this is *so* Broadway."

"Off-Broadway."

Sunny laughs. "Are you good to go? I just came down to tell you to break a leg. You're a star, you know that? You're a legitimate star."

A couple of my castmates go by the door outside, chanting their last warmups together. I should be out there with them, and there's a tug at the base of my spine —go, *go*.

"I'll be good once I get out there." With every moment that Summer stands in front of me, the evening comes into sharper focus. I'm about to step onstage on opening night. In front of real people. My stomach twists. "You might want to stand farther away. Now that you're here, I want to throw up."

"Oh, don't do that. Your makeup is flawless."

I glance back into the mirror. "My makeup is stage makeup. Sunny, I know you say these things with love, but I'm really going to be okay."

"Okay? You're going to be *amazing*. I'll be right there in the front row, cheering and clapping *way* too loud." She takes my hands in hers and squeezes. "I'll get out of your face. But I hope you know you're my best friend. And I'm so proud of you."

It sends a warm glow through my chest. "Thanks, buddy."

Summer precedes me out of the dressing room and we almost run into the stage manager, Joe. "One minute," he barks at me, as if I'm not the star of the show. "Let's move. *Move.*"

I move.

The moment I'm in the wings, in the dark backstage, clasping hands with Jason, all the jitters go out of my soul.

I sit there in it—the ache. The ache of knowing he won't be there. The ache of knowing that Summer and Day still came out to see me, to cheer me on. And the hope. God, that little dancing flame of hope. I can't stamp it out, even though I know it'll only end in desolate crying on my bedroom floor later tonight.

The announcement about cell phones plays over the loud-speakers. Jason squeezes my hand. The music swells from the orchestra pit and I breathe in the dusty backstage, breathe in the air, weighted with anticipation.

Three, two, one.

That's my cue.

I step onto the stage, into those lights, and I'm not Whitney Coalport, recently abandoned and smarting with pain. I'm Holly Hamilton, a woman about to set foot in the big city, destined for love. In fact, it's a love that prevails, despite some real fucking low points in the show. That'll show me. Someday, *someday*, I'll have a love that doesn't leave me wrung out and ragged, desperate for more.

We move into the first act. Singing. Dancing. I feel completely dropped in. I'm in that magic space when the play is real. When I see Jason's face for the first time, it's *really* the first time, and I gasp a little at the sight of his cut cheekbones in the spotlights. To Holly, he looks like an angel sent from heaven. He lights her on fire and I feel it down to my fingertips. Down to my *bones*.

It's so real, even the singing, that I don't look out into the blinding lights. I don't look down into the audience, even at the first row, which is about all I can see when the stage lights are up.

I just don't look.

Not even at intermission, when the curtain drops down beneath me and I'm abruptly shoved back into the real world.

Twenty minutes of the real world, anyway. I can hear Summer screeching her cheers on the other side of that thick velvet curtain, but not Wes.

"That was fucking amazing." Jason's face swoops in close, a fine sheen of sweat over his features. "We gotta bring it for the second act."

Rowan rushes in too, her eyes wide and shining. "This is going *very* well. The critics in the third row nodded several times during Act One. Whit—come with me. There are a couple things I want to tweak…"

She talks for the next twenty minutes. I don't even have time to pee. Ah, but what are human bodily needs when there's a show to put on? What's a full bladder when it comes up against the eternal glory of getting a good clip in tomorrow's *Post*?

One moment, I'm singing the opening to the second act and the next moment, we're breaking up. Jason and me. Our characters are breaking up in the show, and God, it hurts. It *hurts*. His words burrow into me like spears and my throat almost tears on mine.

"Don't you see what I've done for you?" My own arrow flies true, wounds him, and I get a strange satisfaction from it. I wanted to wound Wes that night for walking away from me, and I never got the chance.

But Jason doesn't walk away. "What you've done for me?"

"Yes. Everything I've done. Don't you see?" I raise my hands to the city set around us and take a big breath, cheating toward the audience. "Don't you see how beautiful we've made it?"

"You want to know the truth?"

"What's the truth? Tell me, now, before I walk away."

"All I see is you."

He kisses me.

It's the most romantic fucking thing in the world, except for the fact that he tastes like stale Trident and nerves, and the shape of him is all wrong. I lean in anyway. I lean in and there's a collective gasp from the audience, and then the clapping starts. Whooping. Cheering. The sound breaks into the fantasy I'm living in here onstage.

There are two more numbers. One of them is a wedding scene. And then there's us, in real life, arguing in the kitchen. Good-naturedly. The show ends on a gentle note. Gentle, and powerful, and lovely.

Then a burst of music—a burst of applause. The curtain plummets toward the stage, then sweeps back up, and I am all joy, except for a black pit of despair where my heart should be. I can't avoid it now. I can't avoid looking at the first row.

The rest of the cast bows first. That's how it goes—groups of two and three, the main chorus, everybody. They all go first. Does the music always play so *fast*? Jason strides downstage, waves, bows. My throat sears with happiness for him—the audience is loving him. *Loving* him. His parents are right in the front row, along with his younger sister.

He turns, his hair ablaze in the light, beaming, and throws his arm out wide.

It's my turn.

I feel it, but I don't let it show—that last urge to turn and run, into the curtains, into the backstage, and away from all of this. Away from that empty seat. I can't face it. But I have no choice. It's opening night, and this is my final bow.

I keep my eyes toward the back of the house, the applause reverberating off the concrete walls backstage and filling my ears. It's warm under the lights, so warm, but that cold pit of fear at the bottom of my stomach anchors me to the stage, my feet heavy.

I bow.

I take Jason's hand.

We bow together, and I raise my head and I fucking forget.

I forget not to look at the front row. I forget the dagger of pain that's been hovering over me, waiting to strike.

There are three empty seats.

And in the very center, with an enormous bouquet of flowers, all alone, stands Wes.

Looking at me.

My heart shatters and the pieces fly out into the far reaches of my soul and back again. There are hot tears on my cheeks —where the hell did those come from?

"Wes," I say, even though I know he won't hear over the orchestra and the surge of applause.

"Whit." I see his mouth shape the word. I see the set of his jaw. I see the ferocity in his eyes.

And the next thing I know, he's gone.

32

WES

SHE'S the only person in the entire world.

Whitney, dark-haired and elegant, and so *alive* under the stage lights that she looks like she could burst into flames at any moment. My hands are steady around the heft of the bouquet, but my stomach rolls and dives.

Dayton took his fucking phone out the moment the curtain call started. He looked at the screen, whispered something to Summer, and got the hell out of there. I can hear her, somewhere off to my right, her voice the only recognizable thing in the hellish cacophony of the applause. It rockets off the wall of the stage and bounces back over me. I don't turn my head to search for Summer. Whitney's all that I need.

It's too loud—it's tearing me apart—but that asshole shrink I met this morning walked me through a sheet of things to do like I was five years old. The worst part is, that bullshit is already working. It's tenuous around the edges. The thunder of applause threatens to blur into the low rumble of that IED tearing through the tank, again and again.

Focus on the here and now.

Whitney's eyes glow darkly in the stage lights, her costume hugging every curve. She's breathing hard, like she just finished running, and her body leans toward me, even as she keeps her back straight and chin up. Her eyes burn, and I let them capture me, pull me away from the sound. I breathe in deeply. *Your brain doesn't know the difference between fear and excitement.* The bouquet is solid in my hands, the stems still vibrant beneath the tissue paper it's wrapped in.

"Come on up." The voice comes from far away and I have to tear my gaze from Whitney's. It takes every effort, but I know they're talking to me—somehow, I *know*. A short woman, dressed all in black, she's beckoning me to a low flight of stairs at the edge of the theater. Access to the stage, hiding in plain sight. She's smiling so widely at me, and I go. I go to the stairs and she puts a hand on my shoulder. "For Whit, right?" Her words blur together. *Must be Wes. Make her night.* It must be Rowan, Whit's director.

The crowd noise shifts.

"Hold it," Rowan calls to someone behind me. People are getting ready to leave, gathering purses and programs and talking to each other. Whitney stands at the front of the stage, a smile still on her face.

But her forehead is wrinkled.

Her eyes dart from seat to seat.

She's looking for me, and trying to make it look like she's not.

It takes everything I have not to run across the stage to her.

No. I walk. I keep it under control. At the last moment, she whispers, "Oh, Jesus," and she turns, and those same dark eyes sear into mine.

One instant, and her face lights up. It's just like the sunrise —one moment, the world is murky and gray, and the next, color spills into every corner. Color blooms across her cheeks and her hands fly to her mouth.

"You—" The tears come next, welling up. "You still mad?"

"Whitney." The words are impossible to contain. The way she makes me feel—that squeeze, that ache that fills my entire chest—it's beyond measure. "I love you. I'm so fucking sorry. And I brought you flowers."

She flies into my arms then, pushing the bouquet that I've spent the last two hours tending to out of the way. She presses her face to my neck and holds on tight.

Everything falls away.

The chatter from the crowd.

The rush of the other actors and actresses across the stage.

The orchestra, playing the audience out.

There's nothing but Whitney's voice, her scent, her breath against my cheek, and then—

Her lips against mine.

She kisses me like I'm the only thing keeping her on earth, and who knows? Maybe I am. But she's doing the same for me. Without her...

I can't think of my life without her.

There's a sound like the beginning of rainfall. It's soft, in the distance, like raindrops in the forest, and I surface from Whitney's kiss to realize that people are clapping.

For us.

My grip tightens on the bouquet. I can't bring myself to let go of her. I know it must be unprofessional as fuck, but I am lost in her eyes, in her touch, and she's the first person I've ever found who can hold me. All of me. Even the broken, shattered parts. "I'm going to get you in trouble."

She puts her hands on my face, her soft palms against the rough stubble there. "I swear to Christ, Wes, if you ever leave me again—"

"It'll be the end of me." The air scorches my lungs. "I'm done being without you, Whit. One week was all it took. I'm a fucking broken man."

She nips at my bottom lip, audience be damned. "Sometimes, we must be broken, so that our spirits can find new ways to—"

I lean in and press my lips to the creamy skin at the curve of her neck. "Break me again, if that's what you want. I'd rather be torn apart at your hands than live without you."

"That's—" Whitney shudders underneath my hands. "That's kind of gross, Wes." I freeze. Have I fucked this up again? Then Whitney laughs, and the tension flies out of me. "I'll do better. I promise."

"At breaking me?"

"At being—you know, predictable." Whitney looks up into

my eyes and someone in the front row screams, *Kiss her again!* "I can be calm. I can follow whatever routine—"

I take her face in my hands and the bouquet drops to the stage floor. "Listen to me now." She goes still, her hands pressed up against mine. "I don't want you to be calm. I want you to be *mine*. Do you hear me? I love you. *I love you.*"

"I love you," she whispers.

I can't help myself—I lean in one more time. I'm not the kind of guy who takes orders from anyone. I'm the kind of man who gives orders. But I relent. I let her pull me in and I devour her, right there in a crowded room, where anything could happen.

Anything at all.

EPILOGUE

WHITNEY

"ONE MORE SWEEP, and then I'll be good to go."

I tap my foot at the door to our apartment and try to tamp down the excitement sparkling in my veins. It's *unreal*. It's so powerful that it's almost making me irritated.

"Wes, you've done five sweeps. We're ready to go. We can buy anything we forgot on the road. Plus, aren't we meeting Ben before we go?"

He appears from the bedroom, an easy grin on his face. "No rush. Ben texted. He's got other plans in the city. Some woman he met, I guess?" He raises his eyebrows. "You, on the other hand... You look like you're trying to hurry me along. You look like you *really* want to get out of here. It's like you want me to cut corners." Three long strides across the entryway and he's swept me up in his arms. Hot *damn,* he smells good. It doesn't matter how long we live together. I'm never going to get over the intoxicating, manly scent of him, like leather and a clear day. He takes my bottom lip between his teeth and holds it there for a long moment.

Things have been relatively calm since the whirlwind that was opening night. The image of him standing there onstage, flowers in his hands and *sorry* on his lips, is burned into my brain. In a nice way, I mean. And afterward? Wes and I went back to my apartment—*our* apartment—and he told me everything. How the explosion had haunted him. How it had wrapped tighter and tighter around his mind until he couldn't escape it. How the guilt—*guilt*—tore him in two, and it was only his last-ditch attempt at talk therapy that finally pulled him out, and back to me. It was not easy, sitting in that theater. My heart squeezes thinking about it. We talked until four in the morning, and then...

Well. You know what happened then. A guy spills his heart out like that? With a face like Wes's? Don't even get me started on his *body*.

"Oh, fuck," I say into his mouth. "You can't do this to me. I'm *dying* to get going."

He puts me down, my feet making contact with the floor. My heart pounds. "You are absolutely right, love. Except for one thing."

"What's that?"

"You forgot something in the bedroom."

I *tsk* at him. "There is *no way* I forgot anything in the bedroom. For one thing, I've been playing along with this little planning obsession of yours for five days. Everything's practically labeled. And it wasn't *me* who made us stay up last night to double-check that everything was—"

Wes pulls something from his pocket, presenting it to me on the palm of his hand.

It's a little velvet box.

Black velvet.

A deep flush of happiness rockets from my toes all the way up to the top of my head. "That's—"

"That's a ring box," Wes finishes for me, looking down at it like it's so commonplace, to be holding a box like that in his big hand. "In case you were looking for clarification."

"How could I—" I swallow down an expansive joy so I can get the words out. Holy *shit*. I didn't realize I'd feel like this. I didn't know it would be like sprouting wings and flying away on a warm updraft. It's so amazing that I feel slightly wine-drunk, and we're not even close to Vino. "How could I forget something like that? With all your careful planning? Weren't, you know, weren't you the one who was supposed to—"

"I wasn't going to give this to you here." Wes is fighting off a grin, and when he stops fighting, it's the most beautiful thing I've ever seen. "But sometimes it's good to be spontaneous. Someone I love taught me that."

Tears. Tears in my eyes. In all my life, I never thought I'd be the kind of woman who dissolved into tears at her own proposal—if that is indeed what this is—but here I am, my vision blurring. I blink them back. I can't believe he's doing this. I can't believe how far he's come.

How far *we've* come.

"Marry me," I blurt out. "Wait. Stop. I'm sorry. I thought I'd throw in a twist, and now I've completely squashed this moment like a little bug under my heel—"

Wes raises one thick finger and presses it against my lips.

"Whitney Coalport," he says solemnly. "I've loved you since the moment I slammed that door in your face."

"Highly romantic," I say around his finger, the words muffled.

"And if you would shut up for two seconds, you would get to hear that I never want to spend another day of my life without you. Even if that means baking in the middle of the night. Even if that means the occasional surprise vacation."

I want to crack a joke about how everyone loves baking in the middle of the night, and how the midnight cake incident was *one time*, but my throat is tight with wonder and love. The Wes who shut that door on me wouldn't have gone on a surprise vacation in a million years. Not that *this* vacation is anything like a surprise—he's been planning the trip for three months.

That's Wes.

"You're the only one I want to ruin my plans."

I wrap my arms around his neck and kiss him. It's deep and lingering and by the end of it, I'm surprised to find that I'm still wearing panties.

Wes looks into my eyes. "Is that a yes?"

"That's a *hell* yes." He gathers me into his arms again, and I lay a hand against his chest. His heart is pounding, jumping against his rib cage. "Oh, my God, are you okay?"

"Never better." Wes shoves his hand back into his pocket and grabs the final bag from the floor. Our suitcases are already in the car downstairs. All that's left is a duffel bag of our road trip essentials. It's been packed for a week—the last chargers went in this morning, along with the other tidbits we keep on our nightstands.

He takes my hand and heads for the door.

"Hey. Don't I get to see the ring?"

Wes laughs. "I thought you liked to be surprised."

"I like to be surpris-*ing*. There's a difference."

"I'll be in charge of the ring." He withstands my good-natured harassment all the way to the elevator bank and steps inside. "Ground floor, please."

I lean down to push the button for the ground floor and when I straighten up, there it is. Nestled in the open box, atop Wes's palm. A thin silver band, gleaming from its perch, and a solitaire diamond. It takes my breath away.

"Surprise," he says.

"I love you, too. Are you going to let me wear it?"

He lets out a breath. "I think I have to, now that you've seen it." Wes slips it onto my finger while the elevator glides downward, toward earth. It's a perfect fit. Goose bumps race from my fingers over my shoulders, down to the base of my spine. I have a *ring*. Oh, my God, I have Wes's *ring*.

He puts an arm around me and presses a kiss to my temple. The elevator glides to a stop and the doors open. For once, I'm speechless.

"There's one more surprise."

"What is it?"

"I'm going to let you pick the route." He turns me toward him, puts two fingers underneath my chin, and raises my face to his. "Do your worst, Whitney Coalport. You want to take us to the ends of the earth, I'll follow you."

I think of all the nights he's spent hunched over his laptop, comparing hotel destinations and traffic patterns, and I can't do it. "You know what? Let's not. Let's do everything according to plan."

The way he kisses me then is completely off-script.

"Okay," he agrees. "Let's give it our best shot."

AUTHOR'S NOTE

Our hero Wes Sullivan is a creation of my imagination, but his struggles with PTSD reflect reality for many veterans and servicemembers. One of readers suggested that I include information about the Veterans Crisis Line here for anyone who might need it—endless thanks to you, Ramona.

If you are a veteran or servicemember in crisis, or are the friend or loved one of a veteran or servicemember in crisis, please consider contacting the Veterans Crisis Line. They are available 24 hours a day, 7 days a week, 365 days a year via phone, online chat, or text.

Call 1-800-273-8255 (Press 1)
Send a text to 838255
Chat at veteranscrisisline.net

For more books by Amelia Wilde, visit her online at
www.awilderomance.com

Made in the USA
Middletown, DE
27 July 2022

70105871R00159